OZMANDER

BOOK ONE OF THE WOVEN WORLDS

A NOVEL OF EPIC HIGH FANTASY BY

LUKE TAYLOR

ISBN 978-0-9906249-9-8

Cover design by Laura Gordon
Metrica Font by Oliver James
Map by Luke Taylor
Proofreading by Amber Hetchler

Also by Luke Taylor
Evening Wolves
The Quiet Kill
Shatterpoint Alpha
The Muiread
Vault of Dreams

GLOSSARY

CRAFT – Magic
SANCTUS – Spirit
TEMPUS – Body
MYSTIS – Mind
GYYD(S) – God(s)
SYR – Sir
HEX – Curse
FEYA - Fairy
PRYYSTYS – Priestess
PALADYR – Paladin
WOVEN WORLDS – The interconnected multiverse
SOLDYR – A soldier not yet achieving rank of Paladyr
COVEN – Covenant, a blend of mind, body, and spirit
NOMYD – Nomad, a travelling healer
LEARNYD – Learned, a sect of scholars
INFERNIUM – A sect of anti-CovenCraft warriors
SHUKACH – A wandering protector/guardian

THE WEST

Lost Woods

Shadow's Edge

ELVEN REAVE

The Silent Trees

WESTERN CREST

Ramzalidun

Kulishkayh

EASTERN SPINE

The Great Steppes

Ruins of Kurayh

Sarmansk

THE WILDS

Forest of Eternal Winter

The White Rush

The Blue Rush

Zumuridon

The Temple of Thanem

DWARVEN REAVE

The Haunted Trees

Perisaris

SEA OF THE SETTING SUN

The Tusked River

The Pyramids

Pits of Ulen

DWARVEN CREST

The Kh'Sala

The River Iklen

Zaminaris

Kalazaris

Forest of Wraiths

GIANT'S FIST

Komoridon

Nazarudara

The River Scourge

SEA OF SALT

The Isled River

DOOM'S CREST

Trees of Midnight

GIANT'S EDGE

Rayh

Desert of Pale Bones

Utzharis

Ruins of Kazimayh

OZMANDER

PROLOGUE

The women sat in a circle before the altar, firelight throwing shadows across the sandstone walls of the temple.

Eyes closed, bodies still, a low hum drifted from their throats, like the hushed drone of distant bees.

"To the Gyyd of the Sea, we give salt."

Bluish sparks ran through the fire as the High Pryystys tossed a handful of dried minerals into the flames. Sweat trickled down her brow from the intense heat, her face glazed and wet.

"To the Gyyd of the Sky, we give tears."

The clear contents of a crystal vial splashed from her hands. The fire roared.

"To the Gyyd of the Trees, we give bones." Two pale white twigs with papery bark were consumed. "And to the Gyyd of the Earth, we give blood."

The censer was a thin golden bowl, placed between two hands of stone. Outstretched, palms up, the fingers of each hand were carved in the faces of the Gyyds. Wystaer and Taerus, of Sea and Sky, Tornim and Tongus, of Sun and Moon. On and on in the manner they had revealed themselves to humankind. Day and Night. Man and Woman. Life and Death.

The Pryystys squinted as the ritual continued, the fire hotter than ever before as each and every ingredient built upon itself to a point of climax. Deep within, she felt as if the flames themselves were alive, speaking to her with a voice she did not hear but *understand*.

As the tenth offering entered the fire, white sparks leapt and the flames nearly touched the shrouded face of the altar's bust. The Pryystys kneeled and moaned, bowing again and again as the other women in the circle behind her followed. The roar of the fire increased in their ears, their voices mounting with its sun-like radiance, till the Pryystys stood up.

"Bring the children!"

Two babies were brought to her, not more than a month old. Swaddled in silks as pale as their skin, they were delicate and angel faced. Wisps of blonde hair curled above their heads, and their eyes were wide in searching the many sandstone pillars of the temple, the dancing of the shadows, the bowing bodies of the bejeweled Pryystyses and the unseen face of Thanem, Gyyd of the Woven Worlds, his immense stone bust shrouded and blackened with smoke. Of all these things, the one that caught their newborn eye was the fire.

One started to cry.

The other remained silent. Resolute. He squirmed and squirmed, but the Pryystys held him close and tight to her chest. He was the strong one. She would offer him last, after the cries of his blood brother had been quenched in flames.

"And to Thanem!" The Pryystys' voice rose to a shout. "Gyyd of the Woven Worlds, we offer these children! Hatebreed of the Dark Lord Ozmander!"

The weak babe wailed and the Pryystys opened her eyes to see him safely to death in the censer.

But a dark silver shadow stood tall at the back of the room.

Her breath caught in her throat and she hugged the children close.

"Who are you?"

The figure descended the stairs one at a time, spreading his cape as he did. It was sapphire silk, and his silver armor shone in the firelight. By the time he'd taken the stairs, a slender blade was in his hand, its length etched with runes.

"By what right do you murder these innocents?" His voice was an animal growl, torn from a silver helm.

No flames could melt the ice on the High Pryystys' beautiful face.

"I am their mother."

The man looked at the other women in the circle, and a tense moment passed between them until the man spoke again.

"I cannot allow it."

"And who are you?" The Pryystys sneered, veins popping from her neck. "Who are you to tell me what I can and cannot do?"

"I am Paladyr of The Infernium. I am the Law."

"Paladyr." The Pryystys snarled. "So you have lost your own name to take theirs? Paladyr. You're *all* Paladyr. You have no soul. No Sanctus. You hunt me and my sisters down and butcher us like cattle. But I say you are the enemy, *not* us."

Paladyr took a step forward. One of the women in the circle tensed, her eyes wide. Brown-haired and soft boned, no one would've known just by looking at her what sort of power she could wield.

But Paladyr knew.

"Give me the children or prepare yourself to die." The Holy Knight growled, barely unable to contain his rage.

The High Pryystys flared her nostrils.

Her brown-haired sister jumped to her feet and threw a spiral of blue light from her hands. Paladyr slashed at it with his sword but it caught him off balance. The Pryystys rushed to complete the ritual, speaking words in the Gyyds' Tongue as fast as she could. The weak babe wailed and the strong one squirmed, reaching out to grab her blonde hair.

Paladyr cut through two of the women with ease. They fell without a fight. Three more threw themselves at him, their Craft failing to his. Finally it was up to the brown-haired Pryystys, her doe eyes and small stature deceiving, as she blocked his sword blows with a staff of hexed wood just as strong as steel.

But it was of no use.

Paladyr was the finest of The Infernium. The finest of all those who believed in human beings, not Gyyds. Those who saw practitioners of CovenCraft as enemies of human kind, fit to be culled and slaughtered.

Paladyr leveled his blade. The killing had grown silent. The Pryystys was alone with the roar of fire and sharpness of her own breath. Her last breath.

"You had your chance." Paladyr said.

Tears fell freely from her cheeks.

"But they are children of the Dark Lord Ozmander! They must not be allowed to live! Evil will they bring upon the land! Death and curses and destruction just as he!"

Paladyr shook his head as he sheathed his sword.

"That is their choice. Not yours."

The Pryystys didn't fight as Paladyr took the children, easily holding them both in the crook of his left arm.

With his right hand, he grabbed a handful of her hair and twisted. The Pryystys sank to her knees, whimpering.

"Is there no pity in your heart? Not for me, but for the world? They will most surely be twice the hellions that Ozmander was. You must *not* let them draw another breath."

Paladyr bent down to whisper in her ear.

"I will always pity the children. But never the one who birthed them."

And with that, Paladyr tossed the High Pryystys into the golden censer, and held her still as she thrashed and screamed, the heat barely warming his silver armor. He watched as she burned alive, withering like the leaves of autumn, until the rigid frame of her black bones was frozen still beneath the hooded stone face of Thanem, hands outstretched to receive the offering.

Paladyr stared at the giant carving of the Gyyd, each of the fingers staring back at him, their tips carved into a different face. He lifted his silver helm just enough to glare at the altar, spit, and turn his back, walking up the temple steps.

Outside in the chill, the cries of newborn babes pierced the silence of the night.

ONE

I found him near the trees, just beyond the path to Kalazaris. Face down, I could see the rose petal pink of his flesh, woven in snow. One arm was buried in a lumpy drift, the other stretched on the ground before him, out toward the horizon. I looked around for something that would tell me who he was and why he was left abandoned just a pace or two off the well-traveled road to the Great City of Sin, but the day was as silent as it was cold.

It was just me and him.

The sun was a red orb, low in the cloudless sky, tinting the snows far and wide across the vale with blood. Pine hills edged the corners of my vision, ahead and behind, wolven eyes woven deep into their dark thickets.

So I was faced with the choice.

To help or to heal was my greatest aim. In all things. A lofty aim. Ambitious, even. If only it worked out that way. The Learnyd had a way of making it all sound so simple, stuffed behind the shelves of their libraries. Voices droning over the crackle of hearth fire. Endless discussions of ancient tomes. Tests, tests, and more tests. Lectures. Tests. Lectures. Tests.

Discipline.

But out in the frozen wastes between citadels it was a different world. Every word forgotten, every missed question rendered meaningless. Mocked by the low-hanging red sun and the snow. By the vastness of life.

By the emptiness of the Nomyd path.

Nomydry proclaimed *one who was once hurt must learn to heal.* But if the man was dead, my choice had already been made for me.

I set my satchel down beside me and stretched out my hand. His skin was hot to the touch and while I wondered at this, he began to stir, as if he'd merely fainted. Gyyds knew how long he'd been there, alone, and what'd happened to put him there. As he stirred I stood tall and took a step back, watching him come to life as if it'd been my touch alone that had woken him.

I squinted as he moaned and pressed himself up. He was shirtless but his breeches were simple white wool, his feet still lost in snow. Watching as he broke free and took a few steps toward the red orb of the low sun I could not help but think I'd stumbled upon something gone wrong.

Had someone robbed him? Sought to kill him? Did some disagreement take place that saw him drugged and left for the winter winds to make a corpse of? Some offering for the black wolves of the thickets to fight over?

Or had some form of CovenCraft stripped him of more than just his tunic, but his Mystis as well? One could never know.

Nomyds had to be ready for anything.

TWO

He noticed the red sun first, and me second. The sun with misty eyes, as if seeing a long lost lover, and me with disgust, wild and untamed.

"Who are you?" He said, his stupor not yet broken.

"Who are *you*?"

He wobbled. I reached out a hand for support and he slapped it away with inborn reflexes. His hand had become a knife, and with the snow's chill and the deadness of the world, his touch stung me.

I took a step back.

He stared as he stood rigid, eyes black as night fixed on a spot of snow. Perhaps his Mystis was locked in a struggle for possession of his body. Perhaps he was trying to remember. Lost in the shard of a moment. Recalling the last thing that came to him before the black of the void took its place. Either way, he inhaled sharply and his stare drifted my way.

"I'll ask you again." He said. "Who are you?"

He was a slender man, terribly forgettable save the deadness that sat in his eyes. It was paralyzing, to say the least. To look at them was to fall into them, like the mouth of a cave, and I was compelled to answer him for reasons I'll never remember.

"I am Rosalyn, a Nomyd from Bayh Creek. I am on my way to Kalazaris."

At that he laughed. He laughed like I've never heard a man laugh before, with thunder that shook my bones. His slender body was possessed by the fit, for a moment, and then he wiped his eyes. His tears were like crystals.

"How old are you?"

I tensed.

"I told you my name. Please Syr, tell me yours."

"How old are you?" He said again, still unwinding himself from the laughter. Still wiping his eyes with his thumb and forefinger.

"Fifteen years."

He rubbed his chin thoughtfully, and in doing so, realized he was without a tunic.

"Fifteen, huh?" He looked around carelessly for it and let his eyes find mine again. "Isn't that a bit early to be peddling your beliefs in the City of Sin?"

"You know of the Great City?" I said, trying very hard to sound friendly. Mockery was written all over his face. His thin eyebrows and needle-like nose. His sharp cheeks and chin. The little black nubs of his hair, and the shadow of a beard on his face. And as his black eyes drank me in, I felt smaller and smaller and smaller in his presence.

"Everyone knows Kalazaris, little lady. Everyone and *everything*."

Thin lips curled in disgust and he twisted away from me to stare again at the red orb, low in the cloudless sky, streaking blood across the snow.

"Do you need any assistance?"

When he didn't answer I cleared my throat.

He cut me off to say he heard me the first time and he sat down on his haunches, peering into the distant red light. He did this for several moments. It seemed like much longer than it truly was.

Even then I wished to know his thoughts. But my Mystis was untested in the vast wastes of life, dulled by the academics of The Learnyd. Taught to remember, *not* to ascertain. I thought what they told me to think, and said what they told me to say. My Mystis was full of information, none of it meaning too much in the moment.

And so I waited, ignoring the one thing that mattered the most.

Quietly, there was a voice inside of me that told me to run. Deep in my Sanctus. Nothing more than a whisper.

Run.

Run to the wolves if I had to.

They would be a lot safer.

THREE

Night fell quickly as we walked, the sun growing darker with every step. Blood turned to wine, purple like a bruise.

"You still haven't told me your name." I said.

"Does it matter?"

"Yes."

"Names change. People do not." He mumbled. "Call me what you will, you won't know me for long."

I ground my teeth at his callousness. Didn't he know Nomyd Creed? Or did he know it all too well and was trying to ruffle my feathers? Was he trying to lose me? Get me to walk off, all frustrated?

He was doing a good job of the latter but I held rigid to my teachings and told him anyway.

"When one saves a life one is bound to keep it."

"Nonsense."

"But that is responsible!"

"No, not that part." He smiled. "The part about saving my life."

I frowned at him.

"You were left for dead."

"It takes a lot more than snow to kill me, little lady." His black eyes caught a purple twinkle from the sun. "You *didn't* save my life."

"My name is Rosalyn."

"You didn't save my life, *Rosalyn*."

"I didn't?"

"No." He squinted at the sun once more as the path began to snake through rocky terrain. Sharp stones pierced the skin of snow blankets like the broken shields of forgotten battles.

I hugged myself, suddenly feeling cold. The trees were nearer than ever. Dark and thick. The garments of my Nomydry were nothing more than oversized woolen breeches and a pair of dusty tunics made of thin cloth. Both my cape and boots were patched leathers.

"So what...you were just...*resting*?"

"You could say that." He inhaled the cold air. "It's a lot cheaper out here than in one of those big cities you're so quick to run off to. It's beautiful."

"What about the wolves?"

"What about them?"

I hitched up my satchel. It felt heavier than it was. Misunderstanding was weighing me down again. Whenever I didn't get something, I collapsed inward, searching my Mystis for a way to process it. To spread it out and look at all the pieces. To make sense of them.

But the more I thought about this man, the less sense he actually made.

"Are you not afraid of them?"

"City walls? Perhaps. Especially the big citadels. The kind that eat man and beast alike. Wolves? Not at all." His teeth were pale as the sun died in the sky, his skin smooth and glossy. Perhaps it was the light. I remember him looking rougher, not that long ago. Now there was a slick confidence in his steps, as if the darker it got, the freer he was.

The more at home he was.

"Yes, the wolves." I said. "Are you not afraid of them?"

"No, little lady. They are afraid of *me*."

I swallowed as he stopped walking and turned, slowly, to look at me. The purple night sun framed his skull, and he took a step toward me, dipping his chin.

"Aren't *you* afraid of me?"

I took a step back and a sharp stone bit into my foot. "No." I squeaked.

"Why not?"

I never got to answer. A sickened howling rose from the trees. It ran through my blood like a curse. My breath left me.

The man tensed, snapping his gaze to the jagged teeth of the forest just beneath the wounded eye of the night sun. The trees looked closer than they were the last time I checked.

For a frozen heartbeat, he waited, as if to stretch out his Sanctus.

Then he grabbed my arm and pulled me into a run.

"What is it?" I cried, fighting my satchel as it thumped against my side.

The howl twisted across the lonely snow once again and I might've heard the man laugh.

"Not a wolf."

FOUR

Kalazaris seemed to shrink as we ran to it, the oblong shape of its massive walls wriggling like a snake across the snow.

The night sun above was losing the last of its color, fading to black.

I lost my footing as the ground shook. A squeal escaped me as I fell and scraped my hands on the rocks. He had me on my feet in an instant.

"Don't move."

He was gone before I could say a word, and I was left to stare at my hands. Palms that had never seen a day of labor in their life were cut to ribbons. The cold numbed them, and the dark sun of true night colored my blood black as oil.

The ground shook again and the howl tore through the woods. My breath, quick and gluey in my throat, was a cloud before my eyes. I took a few steps forward to find the man. To see where he'd gone to.

He knelt in the snow, just a pace away from me.

I watched in awe as he moved his arms. Gracefully he traced invisible shapes and reached down for handfuls of snow and threw them in the air. He continued to do this as the shaking became so bad I could barely stand. There wasn't much to me as it was, but he seemed unmoved.

I looked to the forest again and back to him, blinking rapidly as a snowflake touched my nose like a cold, wet kiss. Startled, I could see that snow had begun to fall.

But there were no clouds.

It made sense in my Sanctus, but not my Mystis. I knew he was creating a blizzard and watched the weather tense and congeal, the night somehow getting brighter with the fury of the snow. He whipped his arms around and the wind followed his touch, until the snowstorm was so powerful it nearly tore my satchel from my shoulder.

I fell to my knees as the creature broke through the forest in an uneven lope.

To say it was a wolf would be a lie. It was three wolves in one, its body the size of three in breadth and height, all three heads full of gleaming white teeth and yellowy eyes.

But the man was unmoved.

He plunged his hand deep into the snow and began to draw a shape. I wanted to cry out to him, to tell him to run, or to do something. Something that made sense. But again, that was my Mystis. No books could prepare me for this, but the thoughts were all there. The reasoning that, somehow, there was a right and wrong way to handle it, and he was doing neither. Something *rational* had to be done. But what? He *was* doing something. Something far beyond the world in which I lived.

Beyond all that I had grown to understand.

Or at least all that I had some bald old man tell me I had come to understand before sending me out to walk the Nomyd Path, only to realize I knew next to nothing.

Especially of Craft.

But my Sanctus, scared as I was, felt awake and alive in the blizzard. I felt ignited to watch him work. My Sanctus knew what he was doing far before my eyes ever saw it come together. Far before my Mystis could process it.

The three-headed wolf was almost on the man, its giant legs tearing through the snow with ease. Still the man worked, tracing his shape. He would not be rushed.

Carefully the man bent low and blew across the shape he had traced. A glimmer caught the dark light of the near-black sun and he snatched something from the ground.

It was a sword.

A sword of ice, blue-black in the night.

The man had made a sword of ice.

The creature was upon him in a splash of snow and he ducked a snap of teeth and shoved the sword into the jaws of another. The creature snarled and lunged, chomping a giant bite of air where the man had been as he dove to the side.

Tears streaked my eyes as blood ran free on my hands. I blinked them away as the man became a blur, fighting the creature with speed and grace.

I had no idea how he could hurt a three-headed wolf the size of a small house with a sword of ice, but then again I'd never been outside the walls of Bayh before.

Pain gripped me as the swirling snow numbed me.

I thought of the walls of Bayh one last time and passed out, falling across the cold ground.

FIVE

I heard the noises first. The *clang clang* of workmen shaping metals with snub hammers, the clatter of a cheap shield being dropped by a hopeful Soldyr still haggling the price. The whoosh of a smithy, its billows being stoked. Children smacking wooden swords. Donkey carts trotting in barrels of fresh ores for young men to lug them to sorting piles, bantering about anything and everything as they did. Slowly, I opened my eyes and watched as it all slid away.

Upside down.

He was carrying me, and waking up amidst the jostle of people seeking the night's many sins made me sick. I smelled food and perfume and oil and sweat. For every pair of eyes that knifed my way and thought a hundred thoughts, ten more ignored me completely. Dangling over the man's shoulder like a fresh kill didn't help. But maybe that was common practice here in Kalazaris.

How could I know? This was my first visit. And being the bright pupil I was, The Learnyd had sought to make Kalazaris my crucible when seven other much smaller citadels would've worked just fine. They were closer, too. So if anything happened that would send me running back to the walls of Bayh, crying for help, they could easily give it.

Maybe that's why they sent me out to Kalazaris. Because it couldn't have been any further from Bayh. The journey itself couldn't have *been* any more forgettable and mundane. Those without a strong Mystis would've lost it, being alone for so long. Seeing the same wasted terrain over and over and over as the days grew colder. The nights longer.

Had they tried to get rid of me?

The thought drifted across my Mystis like an ugly gray stormcloud.

But it wasn't worth thinking about when so much swirled around me. So many lives and stories. So many histories. The energy of the street made me woozy. It tore the past from my grip, crushing the stoic studies of Bayh like the blacksmith's hammer.

He carried me easily down the main street. Torches cast shadows deep into the alleys as the city gate shrunk and shrunk in my weary eyes. Even as far away as it was, I marveled at the size. It seemed like Bayh itself could sit within the gates of Kalazaris. It made me feel sheltered in my upbringing. Cloistered and locked away from the world around me. A world of a million paths. Not just the Nomyd.

My head throbbed as the man walked and walked. Now it was all looking the same. Muddled and meshing together. Why did it feel like I'd been out for two days?

Had I?

My Mystis was blank and dumb under the rush of voices and faces, many of them painted in garish colors. The confusion of the moment warred against the mystery of the past. I didn't remember anything after seeing the man rush to fight the three-headed beast.

I wish I had, though. I wish I had.

Because I wanted to know more.

My Mystis ached just to think about it. To even consider the world of possibilities just beyond the pages of the books I'd been told to memorize and enact as Law.

My Sanctus leapt inside of me as the man took me down a darkened alley to an Inn aptly named *The End of The Road Inn*, because it was as if I could feel him searching and searching and searching.

And finding.

It comforted me because I wanted to know more about what he'd done back there when I really thought we *had* met the end of the road. To the snow. To the creature I'd never seen before and didn't even know existed. I wanted to know, but it was like I *had* to know. I couldn't sleep until I knew. And my ability to feel him looking with more than just his eyes and listening with more than just his ears told me I wasn't dead to the whole thing.

To something they never talked about at Bayh, like it was a long lost relative exiled from the family.

Craft.

SIX

The common room was a squarish thing of cracked plaster and smoke-blackened wood panels. A few pairs of travellers lingered over cups of mulled wine, their heavy packs next to them on the floor. A shaggy dog with one blue eye and one brown eye chewed on a bone beneath the table near the fire. A tall barmaid with braided hair swirled some herbs and spices in a cup before pouring the contents into a large pitcher. The smell was intoxicating, heavy with cinnamon bark and warmth.

The man caught the eye of the wither-bodied patron, who approached with frailty. Their voices were muted. As if they spoke in code.

I heard the clink of coins and then the man carried me up a flight of stairs, lingered for a moment, as if to search every room on the floor through his Sanctus, peering past all the shut doors to see who was inside of them. Content, he carried me up another flight of stairs to the room he had purchased for me and gently placed me on the bed.

Then he left as if he'd never been there at all. Not even a scent lingered, as if he had removed every trace of ever walking the earth. I forced myself to hold onto the images of him fighting that beast, but the harder I tried the quicker they slipped away. As if they'd never happened.

He probably knew that I had come to consciousness, but I didn't think of that. I waited a few moments before sitting up, rubbing my eyes and coughing away the dryness in my throat.

It must've been two days at least. I could drink a whole river. I thought of the creek that ran just outside of Bayh, and how the water ran clear in the sunlight. My mouth ached with thirst and I wondered why I could recall that little creek so sharp and vivid but not the last few days. At all. Even my road to meet the man was smeared with white snow and sameness. A handful of oats cooked in a cup of melted snow. A few berries. Dark days and slow nights, roasting embers dying slowly in my eyes. I couldn't see anything else in my Mystis. I sighed away my frustration. I had been told by The Learnyd that I'd shaped my Mystis into a weapon with my knowledge by the time I'd graduated studies. Now I was learning that *weapon* wasn't much more than the wooden swords those children had been playing with outside the blacksmithy.

I looked around the humble room, which wasn't much more than the lumpy bed and a table for candles, food, and whatever items the renter wished to place there. There was barely enough room next to the table for a large pack. I looked around for my satchel and didn't see it. It's not like I needed it, but I wanted it still the same and wandered from the room.

I didn't find the man in the hall of either floor, and as I snuck down the stairs I drank in the scene of the common room. I felt myself grow more attuned to the sense of the travellers the less I tried to *think* about them.

There was something about the two with the dog that resonated in my Sanctus as exiles, chased from their true home by far more than sticks and stones.

Yes, it made sense in my Sanctus, where things could exist without reason or explanation. *The End of The Road Inn* was a place for people who didn't want to be found, and currently was full of them.

My eyes passed around the room, watching the barmaid pour a glass of iced milk and set it on the counter. I frowned because no one was there to receive it.

The barmaid then looked over at me.

"Come on." She said.

I shuffled over and sat before her, hunched by the aches in my back from being carried like a sack of potatoes. The cool cup soothed the tender spots in my hands where the cuts had scabbed over.

One sip led to another, and by the time the glass was finished, I sighed, unbelievably refreshed.

"What is this?" I asked her.

A smile was distant in her eyes, her expression vague. As if she was bound to keep a secret to herself.

"It's milk, child."

I scoffed. Not like any milk I had ever tasted. It was as sweet as it was rich, the aftertaste just the slightest bit sour. Every taste made me want another, like a spring flower soaking up the rains.

"From what?"

The voice came from my left. Near the door.

"Dragons."

I hardly recognized the man. A princely cloak of ermine fur was clasped about him with a silver chain. Beneath he wore black leathers, dark as the eyes in his skull, and his narrow features looked dangerous beneath the shiny jet black slick of his hair.

He wasn't just a man anymore. He was something else. Something far more than skin and bone. My Sanctus had been awoken by his, and the knowledge of what secrets slept behind those black eyes of his chilled my spine.

I had no idea what they were. But I knew they were there. Waiting. Brooding, like a slender winter Wight.

I stared at him, wrapped in firelight and fine clothes. Dread washed over me.

Something told me we wouldn't stay long in Kalazaris.

SEVEN

A moment stretched between us and then he turned to leave. It was as if he'd told me everything I needed to know in the space of a silent heartbeat. And if I couldn't get it in that one quick moment then I was a hopeless case.

He was really making me mad. Not only was I still in the dark about his name, and what'd happened back on the road to Kalazaris, he was just going to dump me with the exiles.

At least the milk was good. I felt ready to go back to Bayh and give them a piece of my Mystis.

"Wait." I slipped off the bar stool and ran up to him. "Where are you going?"

He turned slowly, creaking as he did. The leathers smelled fresh and new, and I could tell the fine cloak was too. I wondered if he'd had them waiting for him. And where did he keep the coins he'd paid the owner with? I don't remember him having any coins on him when I found him.

Either way, it was an irreversible truth to me now.

He wasn't just another poor man left on the roadside. The earth was full of them. Strewn across the path of the sun from east to west.

But him? He was a very rare commodity on this earth indeed.

He was someone very *very* important. As important as I was forgettable. We were the complete opposite. Stars above knew why he awoke when I touched him.

But if I knew one thing about him, I knew that was the thing that bothered him about me.

As if he hadn't wanted to be woken and I had for reasons beyond us both.

"Where are you going?" I asked again.

His aura was colder than the blade he'd made to fight the three-headed wolf. And with it he pushed me away. His words were only a formality.

"Where I am going, you cannot."

He tried to leave me again but I grabbed his arm. He stared me down. Growing colder.

"Cannot or should not?" My voice was low for the benefit of the others in the small room, but I'm sure they could hear us anyway. Exiles had better ears than most. The fire crackled over our silence. The dog ground the bone between his teeth.

"Both."

"Then at least tell me what happened back there."

Something wild flashed in his eyes and he drew me aside to the staircase.

"Keep your voice down."

"Then tell me."

"Tell you what? You think too much. You'd never get it. Anything I would say couldn't get past here." He thumped my forehead with two fingers. "And that's the thing that bugs me."

"What? That I woke you up?"

His silence was admittance.

So I prodded further.

"Try me."

The man sighed.

"I don't have time for this." He bit his thin lips and then mumbled out a curse. "I have to meet someone. You can come along but you cannot, under any circumstances, reveal your ignorance. Do you understand?"

I shrugged. How hard could that be?

"But afterward, you will tell me?"

"I can tell you but I can't promise you'll understand."

I nodded, mouth sealed.

"Come on, I'll get your satchel. We have to leave at once. You sure you're up to it?"

"I wouldn't mind a cup of dragon's milk for the road."

I thought I saw him crack a smile.

Or it could've been a grimace.

EIGHT

I wasn't sure how far we'd walked, but my eyes were rolling around my sockets to soak in the night. I saw giants and streetwalkers, men who ate fire and spit it out. Gnomes grilled small birds, feathers and all, in cast-iron braziers and dwarves played games of skill with small tiles. Fortunetellers in pointed hats filled their pockets with half-truths, and dark-skinned elves adorned in shells, bones, and animal skins sold vials of healing liquids. I saw the hard eyes of men paid to kill and the greed of adventurers, glazed in the torchlight, as they searched for danger.

And, above it all, the dimmed windows of the pyramid-topped buildings cast a voyeur's distant gaze over the chaos. The clink of coin was always in my ears, as were hushed whispers and the swish of the man's ermine cloak, whiter than snow, as he walked a pace in front of me.

It felt good to follow him, cutting through the messiness of the streets. I don't know if anyone else felt him in their Sanctus like I did, but power was bottled up inside of him. With every step, his power seemed to grow, as did his focus.

Soon he nearly was the sword he had once made. Frost-bitten so that no eye would dare look his way. His thin features were razor sharp and deadly. His gait was lighter than snow falling on the ground, the swish of his white cloak was narcoleptic. The further we walked, the more the crowds parted far in advance, as if he were a Paladyr with cull orders from The Infernium. Or the basest of glory killers, soaked in blood. Nobody wanted a thing to do with him, and looked past me, too, as a result.

I thumped into him as he stopped. Slowly he turned, his gaze frigid, as if to chastise me for not paying attention. Or to paying *too much* attention to other things. Things that did not matter. Like my thoughts and ideas, rattling around my Mystis.

"You are not, under any circumstances, to reveal your ignorance."

"You already said that."

"I'm saying it again."

"So...you want me to be a mute?"

"That would please me to no end." He muttered, looking down a long alley to what seemed to be a large mansion or temple of some kind, its pillars and doors sitting at the end of the shadows like a gaping mouth. Torchlight glowed beyond like eyes and teeth.

Strangely, we were alone. I hadn't paid attention to our path from *The End of The Road Inn*, but we were nowhere near it.

We were in no man's land. Eerie, as if Kalazaris was abandoned.

I shivered.

He was glaring at me again.

"What?"

"You are *infinitely* out of your depth."

"We've established it already, okay? Geez, why don't you rub it in?"

The half-grimace returned.

"An ogre would have a better chance of wedding one of King Manderly's seven daughters than you grasping what's about to happen."

My sigh was something like an angry cow put to the brand.

"Then why even put up with me? Why not just..."

His eyes were barely visible as he bowed on me, his nose inches away from mine.

"Because *you* know things *I* do not." His voice was a snake-like hiss. "But I cannot, for the life of me, get them from you. Your Mystis is a wall to me. A wall of insects buzzing around in some mad purpose. The answers lie in your Sanctus, but they are buried so far down, I don't even know if they're there, or if I'm just seeing a reflection of my own quest. They must be, or else..." He shook his head. "They have to be. They are. I know it. They're just...locked up within that fortress you call a Mystis. That prison."

His black eyes bore holes into me for another one of those silent moments.

My mouth sagged as he set off for the dark alley and the doors down at the end of it. His white cloak snapped with his swiftness.

For once I didn't know what to think.

He was right. His words had hit my Sanctus with hunger and longing. Like a wayfarer lost in the desert. There was a plea in his anger, desperation in the frustration that I held a secret he needed. It made him vulnerable.

I knew things he did not.

I marveled at the ease of *knowing* this deep down and fought with everything in me not to let that *knowing* slide up to my Mystis to be picked apart and chewed up by all those little buzzing insects he'd said flew around the walls of my Mystis.

I caught up to him, walking quickly.

"We will speak of it later." He nearly whispered.

I gathered it was an apology. As much of one as I'd get from him in the moment. I could tell he was very focused on the task at hand.

"Why not now? Before we go into that..." I pointed. "House thingy, whatever that is. Is it a temple? Opium den? Brothel?"

"It's many things."

"Oh great. That's helpful."

He rolled his eyes and spoke with his teeth grinding together.

"We do not have time to answer your every little question, Rosalyn." He stopped to thump my forehead again. "You have a black hole between your ears." He took a step back, running his eyes up and down my chest. "And a storm between your ribs."

"What's that supposed to mean?"

"Live from your Sanctus, Rosalyn. Shut your Mystis off for once and let that storm in your Sanctus take over. Listen to it howl. Lose yourself in that storm."

I frowned at him.

"You make it sound so easy."

"It is." He said, turning to the glowing torches and pillars once more. "Consider this dangerous task ahead of us as your first chance to see just how much."

I'm sure all of Kalazaris could hear me swallow.

Why did he have to say *dangerous*? I was supposed to be helping people who needed bandages and food. Walking the road and giving water to them that were thirsty. Giving maps to the lost. Making a difference to people others had cast out and forgotten about. That was what I was trained for.

I pressed the palms of my hands into my eyes. Hard.

"I don't like you. At all." I growled.

The grimace returned.

"You're a quick study." He said, and before I had time to respond, I heard the grinding of stone, and took my place beside him as the door slid open like eyelids rolling back to reveal nothing but darkness.

NINE

The darkness receded as we walked, black bleeding to plum to blood red to orange, just like the sun. I wondered at this, but my Sanctus knew it immediately.

Sun cults were uncommon, but not extinct. And this was Kalazaris' very own sun cult temple. The elongated entrance spread like a pair of hands to a round chamber sitting like a dinner plate within a sphere. I'd heard about the architecture of sun cult temples before. They were perfect spheres, hidden behind perfectly normal facades, with moveable shrines for the solstices, and steps for cultists to follow the path of the sun as they prayed and mediated. But the light of the whole temple was artificial. Colors tempered by earthen powders and minerals to reflect the many faces of the sun itself. Or so my study books had said.

I must say, as I watched solemn expressions in long lavender robes, walking around the circumference of the dome with candles and mirrors, I admired their dedication.

The man only stared at me, chilling my spine. I swallowed again and stopped thinking about their dedication, or how they reminded me of Bayh and my studies there.

But subdivisions within The Learnyd scoffed at such believers. Sun cults, moon cults, sea cults. Druidic sects, martial factions. Elven beliefs. Dwarven beliefs. Gnomic beliefs. On and on and on. But then again The Learnyd scoffed at everything they didn't teach.

Craft? That was another thing. They didn't scoff at Craft. They were scared of it. It was the door at the bottom of the ocean. The gate to the cloud steps beyond the mountains. The great unknown they wouldn't talk about. Shouldn't talk about.

Couldn't talk about.

And here I was, the brightest of Bayh's graduates, stuck with someone whose Craft with that three-headed wolf was just the tip of the iceberg.

That I knew. If the guy could bend time, I wouldn't be surprised. Tuck in it his belt like a tunic. Wrap it around his finger and make it float.

"I never expected to see your face again." A man's voice called from our left. The slap slap of soft-soled boots drew the speaker near, and I squinted to study him.

Short and ruddy-faced, his light-brown hair was pulled back and bound, and the beard on his face was neatly trimmed. His leathers were the color of dirt, his tunic of grass, and his eyes of sky.

A bow of honeywood was bound to his back, and four daggers to his chest in a diagonal strap. Each handle was bejeweled with the colors of the sun's faces. Orange ambers, bloody rubies, royal amethysts, and night black opals.

"Nurmedov."

"Xander."

My eyes darted between them both as there was a shake of hands. So the man of mystery, sharp features and black hair I had awoken was named Xander. Xander could Craft heaven knew what and I knew something he didn't. He was going to drag me along some sort of mission of his until he had time to give answers to my questions. And hopefully he was going to exact from me whatever answer I had that he needed. And the walking armory that was looking me up and down as if I was a white-tailed doe in the forest was Nurmedov. Yet another strange man in a strange city with strange eyes. To look at Nurmedov was to see the face of the winter, stripped raw. They were ice. As cold as the aura

Xander emanated. Dangerous as the blade of frost he had made.

Great. Fun stuff. Where's a cup of dragon's milk when you needed it? I felt tired and scared at the same time. And exhilarated. I wanted to watch the sun culters walk and pray but I couldn't take my eyes off of either man. The whole thing was making me dizzy.

There was some history between them. They were birds of a feather, and their last meeting had been cursed with some sort of conflict. The air between them was tense. I felt my Tempus grow rigid. I wanted to shrink into a darker color, but the candles and mirrors bathed us orange.

"Who's she?" Nurmedov said.

"That's not your concern."

"It is if she's coming with us."

"I'm not going with you."

Nurmedov smirked.

"Can't help it old man. You're stuck with me."

"That wasn't the agreement."

"The Infernium cure you?" Nurmedov laughed. "When have you ever kept a promise in your life?"

"Darkness take you." Xander growled.

"And you."

Xander sighed.

"Now I remember why I vowed to kill you the last time I saw you."

"See, you can't keep your promises if you were paid to." Nurmedov laughed. "A year and a day and you're still as sensitive as a mother to be."

"Darkness take you twice."

"It just may where you want to go and you're not leaving without me and you know it. Don't go lone wolf on me now. Not now."

"I wouldn't dream of it." Xander's sincerity was thinner than my understanding of him.

"That's my boy." Nurmedov smacked Xander on the arm, devils may care smirk on his face, and stepped past him to offer his hand. "Pleased to meet you, Mi'lady."

"She's no lady." Xander said before I could open my mouth. Half to say something polite to Nurmedov, half to scream in pain that he'd crushed my hand in his.

"Really?" He stepped back, hands on hips. "She looks ever bit the lady to me. That's if you can see past the knotty hair, dirt-smudged face and the milk stains around her lips."

My cheeks flushed under his gaze. I fought the need to drag my sleeve across my mouth.

"Did you hear about the Zerbrys on the road?"

"Yes I did." He frowned. "Isn't it crazy how The Infernium breed and train those three-headed beasts to hunt CovenCrafters? Not many have the guts or the grit to slay one of them. Nasty business. Wonder what a pelt is worth?"

Xander nicked his chin my way.

"I saw the whole thing. I was on my way here and saw the Zerbrys come out of the woods to get her."

"When was this?"

"Nearly black sun, two days back. She slayed it with a frost blade."

I stood my ground and wondered if I should try to look tough or if that would only give the ruse away. I had no idea why Xander wanted to lie about me to this Nurmedov character, a man who looked to be an adventurer or tracker of some kind, maybe even a tomb-robber or treasure hunter. Either way he was armed to the teeth, carefree, and quite competent. Whatever Xander's reason, Nurmedov eyed me suspiciously for a moment, rubbing his bearded chin, and then broke out in a quiet laugh.

"Well, you know I detest your kind, but sure as sin won't balk at having another one around."

Your kind? Ah yes, CovenCrafters.

Well that made sense. Xander was the enemy. All my life I was told to avoid him. Them. It. The big ugly *it.* Don't look at it. Don't think about it. Don't you dare dream about it.

And if you hear about one or see one or heaven forbid you know one, turn them in to The Infernium to purge. Let the Law bleed the sorcery from their bones. Let the Law inspect them with blades of fire. Let the Law decide what is to become of them. So said the Law.

I sighed to myself.

Since I knew next to nothing about Craft, I had assumed that Xander just knew about it or could use it.

But to say he was a CovenCrafter was to, in one breath, bind him in chains before stoic tribunal boards. To strap his arms and legs to four separate horses in the town square and put the whip to their flanks. To tie him to the stake and watch the Paladyrs light their torches, shiny armor as hard as the eyes behind their helms.

And for me to be labeled as such was much the same fate.

Dread didn't wash over me but seeped through me, making me sick. I stood there, idly, as they talked, fighting to stand straight.

And when Nurmedov rushed off toward one of the many antechambers in the giant sun cult dome, I glared at Xander.

"Thank you very much!!!"

"What?"

"A CovenCrafter??? ME?"

"Shh!" He said, putting his arm on my back, trying to draw me toward the long walk to the door. I shook it off.

"Explain yourself!" He shushed me again and I lowered my voice to a hoarse whisper. "To call me a CovenCrafter is as good as a death sentence."

"It was the only way I could get him to trust you in the blink of an eye."

"A lot of good that does me when I'm DEAD."

Xander rolled his eyes and pulled me toward the long hall to the door. Slowly the colors of the sun bled over us, blending from light to dark.

"Where we're going, The Infernium are no worry."

"We? I'm just waiting for an answer."

"As am I."

"How long do I have to follow you around to get it?"

He merely growled.

My hands went to my head.

"No no no...this is not happening...okay." I sighed. "I just want to know how I woke you up. That's all. CovenCraft, I get. You made a blizzard, you killed a three-headed..."

"A Zerbyrs."

"Yes, a Zerbrys...you killed a Zerbrys with a blade you made...literally out of thin air. That's great. CovenCraft. Cool. Fun. I don't understand it, but I believe it. I know it's true. I just want to know how I woke you up."

We were outside the temple. Again the night was eerie and still.

I felt a headache coming on and looked into Xander's shadowed face. Its thinness and cunning.

"Guess what, Rosalyn?"

"What, Xander."

"We want to know the same thing."

I frowned at him. The truth of it was a thumbprint in my Sanctus.

"You don't know either?"

He shook his head. Behind us, Nurmedov approached with his soft steps. A heavy pack was slung over one shoulder. The man was a mule. I could've fit in the pack with room to spare. Perfect. I could hide in there while everyone in the citadel looked for the young girl who killed the Zerbrys.

"But I will tell you one thing," Xander whispered in my ear, his breath chilly and smelling of mint. "The Infernium breed Zerybrs to hunt for CovenCrafters, right?"

"Yeah?"

"That Zerbrys I killed wasn't looking for me. It was looking for you."

Nurmedov made me jump as he pinched my ear, walking by.

"Come on kiddies." He said, his gait out into the dark alley jaunty. "Market's about to open."

"Market?" I said, still in a haze from the thought of being scented and hunted by such a fearsome creature.

I would've been ripped from limb to limb. Impaled on those fangs.

I shivered to think of it all.

"Where we're going, there's a lot worse things than Zerbyrs, Rosalyn. A lot worse."

He took a step forward, but I didn't.

"Then why take me at all?" I said, half-broken. "I'll only slow you down."

Xander was wounded. I could tell. I could feel it. It was like his bones ached, and his Sanctus was bloody and raw within his belly. Not by me. No, by something far older than me. A lifetime of something terribly wrong that needed to be made right.

He placed his hands on my shoulders and made his voice as soft as he could.

"Because I have no hope of finding what I've been searching for without you."

His hands slid from my shoulders and his feet put distance between us. I wanted to ask a thousand questions but I knew the time for them would come.

High above me, dawn was showing its face. The black sun of night was becoming a purple bruise once more.

TEN

We ascended Kalazaris' inner core as the sun turned red and I was dead on my feet by the time we reached the market. I hadn't slept a good night through since I'd left Bayh. Nurmedov, on the other hand, was nearly bouncing on the balls of his feet, eager to see the dragons.

Breathlessly, through our ascent of Kalazaris, realizing that it was just one giant cinnamon roll with walls, towers, and pyramids, I had asked Xander why we needed dragons.

To cross the sea, he'd told me, with a tone that implied I should've known.

If I'd had the strength I would've asked a question, or thought a hundred thoughts, but I was a quick study. It took energy to use my Mystis. Energy I didn't have. To let a knowing rise up in my Sanctus like the scent of fresh flowers, well, that was like breathing. Or listening. There was no work to it. Since I'd lost consciousness back on the road in that blizzard, seeing things I'd been told weren't true, I felt like my grip on my Mystis was slipping.

I didn't know what to think about that. It was like my Mystis was my reputation. It was me. Or who I'd made myself to be. But it wasn't, was it? It was just a walking library of odds and ends. Nothing personal. Nothing unique. Special. Different. Numbers and dates and languages. I wasn't what I knew. I was something more than that. Something entirely different. What I was...who I was, that was akin to something far more distant in the moment than the stars. Indescribable. Nebulous. But like every star, bright and beautiful and one of a kind. Or so I hoped. I hoped that was the secret of how I'd woken Xander from something I was beginning to think was some very advanced and dangerous work of CovenCraft. I hoped that whatever secret was lurking within me was that I was fine just the way I was and I didn't need to stuff myself with knowledge to prove myself to anyone. It was fine to be me. Whatever or whoever *me* was, that was enough.

And to walk to the very top of Kalazaris felt like a wrestling match between the unknown of who I was to myself and everything I'd built myself to be as the best and brightest pupil Bayh had ever seen. Or so they'd said.

Ascending Kalazaris I'd seen wards and sigils that I knew I recognized, but couldn't place. It made me realize how much I thought I understood behind the cloistered walls of Bayh. It all made sense, there, with three meals much the same and a hard bed. The same old faces and their dusty lectures. Every rule clearly defined and settled, every little fact sealed away as truth in my Mystis. But it all didn't add up, with my feet caught in perpetual motion. Part of me wanted to stop and stare at one of those wards or sigils until I could recall all I'd been taught about the merchant house or royal family such belonged to, but part of me wanted to walk even faster, and leave it all behind. To run away.

It was like I was experiencing the world for the first time, but something in my Mystis told me I had already lived these steps I was taking. I already knew it all. But I didn't. My Mystis was wrong. Deceived by the tomes it'd propped itself up on. Convinced of the truths and laws I'd been handed down by those who may not've even ever been out of the walls of Bayh themselves. Those who may've never even gone out and *lived* life.

I was starting to curse myself when Xander came over to me. We were just outside the largest dragon vendor and its messy sprawl of tented stalls. We weren't alone. Nurmedov was talking to a pair of female merchants in purple wool and just beyond them there were a group of boys that obviously came to the market before school, just to see the dragons and feed them and whatnot. Their cheeks were cheery and red in the frost nip.

"I'll be right back."

"Wait."

Xander stopped.

"..."

I couldn't say anything. I just stared at him and he stared at me.

It scared me.

He stepped closer, shadowing me.

"See, it's not that hard. You know. Don't you? The less you think, the more you know. You know I'm going to go get you some clothes and some more things for our journey, and by *things* you know I mean more than I care to say in the moment, and you know you're going to pick a dragon for yourself, you're going to grow extremely attached to it, and Nurmedov will pick one for himself and one for me."

My mouth just sagged open. It only shut when I swallowed on the count of the dry cold air. I stared at his feet.

"It's all so easy, isn't it?"

He walked away without my response. Good, because I was speechless, and I crossed my arms to think about it. How could it all just...happen? Knowledge was something I'd earned like a stonecutter earned muscle. The fact that my Sanctus could just "know" something made me...well, it made me angry.

It was as if I'd wasted my whole life without knowing it.

Ha! The irony!

"Rosalyn, I want you to meet someone." Nurmedov said as he sauntered up.

I smiled. It seemed Nurmedov's character was not repellent to everyone. Just me. The two female merchants were starry-eyed at his wide smile and his big stories, and I realized it would be a long trip with stony Xander and flippant Nurmedov. With me in the middle, trying to exorcise something that sat just behind my forehead and wouldn't leave me alone.

Their names were Dalys and Darah, both doe-eyed brunettes that looked at me with a strange reverence, as if I were the CovenCrafter I was supposed to be. Not sure how they knew that, other than Nurmedov's mouth wouldn't stop moving. Even to take a breath. We talked with them about Kalazaris until the market officially opened under the great red eye of the sun. Its heat had taken the edge off the chill, but we could still see our breath in little clouds. Nurmedov managed to make everything about himself somehow, and they parted with giving Nurmedov a token of their merchant houses, with hopes of seeing him again.

"What can I say?" He tossed the colored tokens in the air to catch them again as we wove our way through the stalls. Blue-gold for Dalys of Komoridon and red-bronze for Darah of Perisaris. They were both a long way from home. It made me wonder where we were off to. Bayh was long-gone in my Mystis but there were places that I didn't even know about. I'd only studied the maps they had to study. And I wasn't fighting the knowing that there were unmapped places. Lands that lie beyond the vanishing point.

Nurmedov cleared his throat and repeated himself. Obviously he saw me diving into thought again and was throwing me a friendly lifeline.

"What can I say, Rosalyn?"

"About what?" I said.

"Well, you know. Some people are just really hard to dislike."

"If you're talking about me that's very kind of you."

"Rosalyn, there's something you must know about me if we are to travel the world together, seeking fame, glory, adventure, and perfectly smoked cheese."

"What's that, Nurmedov?"

"I have an incurable disease."

"Oh?" I wasn't even going to bother letting my Nomydry rise up. If it was incurable, there was nothing I could do.

Besides, I wasn't supposed to *be* a Nomyd. I was supposed to be a blazing CovenCrafter for crying out loud.

So I remained stoic.

"What's your plight, my friend?"

"It is...that I am obsessed with myself. I can't stop talking about myself and I don't want to. I am the most interesting person I've ever met. The funniest, too."

I couldn't help but laugh.

"The cold fish hasn't cured you?"

"Who?"

"Xander."

"No." Nurmedov smirked, toying with the handle of one of his daggers. The amethyst one. "If anything, his time with me has made him worse."

"Worse? What do you mean?"

"He's incurable, too."

"Hmm?"

Nurmedov sniffed and rubbed his nose. Maybe his eyes were a bit watery.

"I'll tell you after we find our rides. Dragon-buying is an important business. You have to think about size, breed, pedigree, personality. The list goes on."

I nodded. It was a smooth deflection because he was right. To say there were all kinds was an understatement. I had studied dragons at length at Bayh and even taken care of a few in my healing courses. I had assisted with hatching but yet I had no idea why...

I paused, feeling stupid once again. I don't know why it hit me so late.

I'd had dragon's milk at *The End of The Road Inn*...milk came from mammals. Dragons weren't...

I stopped and rubbed my head. I must've groaned. Everything I knew about dragons were contained to egg-laying reptiles. I'd never ever *heard* of mammalian dragons.

Heavens above...

"What's wrong?" Nurmedov said.

"Me."

He scoffed and kept walking.

"Another incurable. You'll do just fine."

He fought the urge to put his arm around me. What a sweetie.

And as we passed through the market I realized that the only way out of this pain I was feeling between my ears would be to shut it off completely, like a man who would no longer use opium.

I had been addicted to my Mystis. Hooked on its power. On the success it'd given me as a big fish in a very *very* small pond.

But now I was seeing just how much it had let me down.

So I vowed to myself I would never trust it again.

I would let my Sanctus buy me a dragon.

ELEVEN

We were almost at the end of the market when I found her, lying on her back.

Nurmedov had since picked out a spirited creature for himself and a long-legged and aloof one for Xander, and was complaining about how it's a crime to be picky and I should be locked away for making him walk so far without so much as a quick diversion to a bakery but I was going to listen to my Sanctus or die trying.

And there she was.

I stepped up to the stall and stood on my tiptoes to study her. Something about her made my Sanctus melt within me.

Lying on her back, her forelegs tucked against her chest, her claws were overly long and twisted. Her fat belly of smooth grey-pink skin rose and fell. Her head was tilted toward me, her little black snout scrunched in deep sleep. What few fangs she had were bared.

"What the…" Nurmedov said as he came up beside me. I shushed him as we listened to her snore.

It was nearly human, the sawing sound of her lungs.

Her black fur, short around her skull, pointy ears, back, and short tail, but long around her skirts, was overly long on her beard, which had gone gray. It was so long it looked as if she'd step on it when she walked on all fours. Her wings were half-tucked beneath her body, one splayed out wide as she slept with the wild abandon of a creature who'd had her adventures and now wanted nothing more than to sleep the rest of her life through.

"She's perfect." I said.

"She's old."

"She's perfect."

"She's fat."

"Perfect."

"Can she fly?"

I shrugged.

"Sure!"

He rolled his eyes.

"*Can* she fly, not *did she fly a hundred years ago*."

"I'm sure she can. She has wings, doesn't she?"

Nurmedov pinched his nose as she sighed extra deep. He frowned at me.

"That breath!!!"

It didn't bother me. Sure it smelled like rotting carcasses but there was something about her I just couldn't leave behind. And I guess that was the point of what Xander was saying about listening to my Sanctus over my Mystis. With my Mystis, there were a thousand options, and I could've spent the rest of my life going from stall to stall, comparing breeds and asking questions and finally convincing myself I made the right choice only to spend the rest of the journey doubting what I'd done.

Wherever the journey was to.

Or I could just listen…to something that couldn't be left behind. That couldn't be ignored. Silent as it was, it just *wouldn't* go away.

It was a connection.

"Go get the handler." I said, staring at her, watching her sleep. There was a heat rolling off of her, probably from her fat belly. It was so fat she must've slept on her back to relieve the weight of it. I wanted to reach out and touch her, she looked so cozy. She was on the smaller side, but then again, so was I. I knew we had to cross the sea, and

Nuremdov's dragon was much bigger. Xander's, too. But she would handle it. I was sure of it.

The handler was an older man whose tunic tented in the back of his slender body as he walked, his gait hunched and quick at the same time. His eyes of dark jade were focused and jumpy at the same time. He was bald and had a thin beard of salt and pepper, and a gold hoop in each ear. The darkened nub of a cigar was wedged in his teeth.

"I'd like to buy this one." I said with a smile. He stared at me for a moment and then tilted his head and said *Arrgh* and leapt into action, getting a ring of keys from a slouched belt on his waist. There was a sense of flair as he flipped them in his hand and released the lock and flipped them back, marching into the stall.

He patted the dragon's fat belly three times and said, "Daisey girl...Daaaaaisey girl!" in a high voice. The dragon kicked her back legs and sat on her side, looking around quickly with big brown eyes, crusted in sleep, blinking and blinking and sniffing until she saw the handler and his ring of keys.

Then the dragon, named Daisey, began to thump her tail on the floor and pushed herself up on her short little legs. Then she skirted the edge of the stall, grinding her body against the wall as she made her way over to the handler.

"Daisey girl...Daaaaaisey girl!"

The small dragon then jumped on her hind legs, hugging the handler and licking his face. He reached down and scratched her back as her tail trembled it was wagging so fast.

I looked over at Nurmedov and smiled. Pain had stretched itself across his face.

"That breath." Was all he said, walking away.

I laughed as the handler continued to scratch Daisey's back.

"A good choice."

I turned to see Xander walking up to me, his sharp features still pensive, but not as burdened as usual.

I shrugged.

"Easy, right?"

He nodded.

"Easy."

But then the smile faded from my face as the unspoken seeped into my Sanctus.

Finding Daisey had been easy.

However, nothing else of what was to come for the both of us would be.

TWELVE

Tall, suntanned, square-jawed, and river-eyed, I recognized him the moment I saw him. I nearly dropped my sweet roll to the cobblestones with the weakness that flooded me. How could two years feel like ten? How could time be so deceiving?

And how could the pain he had caused me be summoned back to the surface in an instant, like a breath of frosty air in my lungs?

"Ilan?"

The man paused and turned to see where the voice had come from. His eyes were sharp and his gaze lingered around the square, studying everything, till it met mine. He didn't look seventeen. Wherever he'd been and whatever he'd done, he looked so much older than when I'd seen him last.

Older and harder.

He spotted me as if it was the drafty dining hall of Bayh once again, and our studies were over for the day. Emotions too clouded for me to make sense of washed over his face.

"Rosalyn?"

"Ilan!" I ran from the eaves of the small bakery where Nurmedov was charming them out of all their piroshki.

He tensed when I reached him. Not knowing what to say. Not knowing what to do. But the fact that I had charged him with a big smile on my face seemed to put him at ease. I couldn't hold onto the pain. Seeing him brought it all back, but each step I took toward him left it where it was. He was different.

I was different.

Still, it was as if there were things he wanted to say, but couldn't. Wouldn't. There was a tic in his jaw. His fists were clenched. He was tenser than a bowstring.

I kept on smiling anyway.

Fine body cast in silver armor, cape of emerald green silk about his shoulders, I think I understood why.

"My name is Paladyr." He said. His once soft voice had gained an edge as if his vocal cords had been put to the grindstone. It wasn't him. Not Ilan. Not *my* Ilan. Someone else, like a character in a play. Not the Ilan I had once known. Those blue eyes of his darted around the square and back to me. They were strained and alert, ready to kill.

"Paladyr?" I said. He didn't have to add *of The Infernium.* The cape and silver armor and joylessness sort of gave it away.

"Yes." He took a step closer and softened. "But I fear I will *always* be Ilan to you, Rosy."

He drew his eyes over my smile, as if to remember better times. I reached out and hugged him and he hugged me back. It was awkward, but I didn't mind. Nothing like the last hug we'd shared. Full of childish tears, I'd sobbed myself dry on his shoulder the day of his leaving Bayh for good. Leaving me alone to brave the rest of my studies with not one friend to my name. As if anyone could ever be the friend he had been to me. But he'd struggled so much with the Nomyd Path and craved something that could do more for the world. Or at least more in his eyes. Something of action. Healing wasn't action to him. Offering a hand wasn't good enough. He wanted to do something *preemptive* and *proactive*. He'd said those words and I had no idea what they meant at the time. Just that I would probably never see him again. Change was burning in his biceps and as a fifteen year old, before graduating his studies, he had felt the call to The Infernium, where they promised to deliver the radical ideas he sought. A place where a hand could form a fist and knock down any wall that stood in its way. A place where swords were aplenty, as were men who served and feared no Gyyds but the ones they became themselves. He was two years older than me, and I looked up to him, but I also knew that The Infernium would ruin his sweet little Sanctus. The boy that I'd come to know as a brother, or at least, the boy who'd let me in past his shell to make me feel like his tagalong little sister, would be no more if he turned his back on Bayh.

On me.

But that was water under the bridge, as they said. Now he was a Paladyr and I was a Nomyd.

"You look good." He held me at arms length. His smile was genuine, and I'm sure I was beaming. "If a bit dirty."

"Aw, you know. Nomyd Path. Don't exactly get palatial house calls much."

"Not what you signed up for."

"Not at all."

He sniggered.

"Palaces are overrated. Life's much more exciting out on the open road."

I bit my lip. *You could say that again.*

He fumbled around for conversation, overwhelmed to see me and trying not to show it.

"Have you...been busy? You know...lots of people to help?"

I couldn't tell him about Xander.

"A few here and there." I said.

"And your travels? It's a long way from Kalazaris to Bayh. Ten weeks by foot, I think."

"You know what they say about a journey of a thousand steps."

A chattering laugh drifted across his smile, but it wasn't the same as it had been. Once loose and free, it was now tight and controlled, as if he remembered what humor was but had none of it to call his own.

"No. I wouldn't know."

"Did you just graduate?" I asked, and only because I had and figured the same of him. Graduations and inductions and employments were all done in cycles and seasons, no matter what citadel or village one called home.

He nodded and my eyes drifted to his sword.

"Paladyrs get a sword when they graduate, right? Warded and all by generational TempusCraft?"

"Yes."

"Well, come on."

"Aw, alright." He said and pulled it out slowly, letting the steel rasp on the hard leather scabbard.

The sun was warming up, but it was still early. Stretching out above the pyramid tops of the buildings, the reddish light gave the sword a hot and hungry glow.

It was long and slender and quick. Runes were scattered down the length of it, as if they'd fallen from the sky. It took my breath away. I couldn't read them, but I'm sure he could and they meant the world to him. Like elven tattoos or gnomic charm bracelets. Everyone had an unspeakable language that could either hide their secrets or show them off to them who knew the same language.

Even me.

A knowing rose up in my Sanctus and it made me shiver.

Secrets? My secret language? That was one of the few things I knew about Craft. That everyone had a secret language given to them at birth.

Some scoffed at it as myth, but others treated it like blood. Like one of the unknown laws of the universe.

I knew what mine was. I knew how I had awoken Xander.

And just to think of him made my skin burn, as if Ilan had come to me just to hunt *him* down. That was my Mystis at work, my Mystis and all of its buzzing little thoughts.

I stowed both my knowing and my crazy thinking away for the moment and scratched my cheek.

"It's beautiful, Ilan. Congratulations."

That much was true. I hated to think of it being leveled toward Xander.

"Thank you." He said. He was still staring at it, as if it was alive in his hand. As if it had its own voice and was whispering to him of the great things they would do together.

He hadn't seen my face when the knowing hit me, or the thoughts that followed.

Thank heavens for that.

"I'm very proud of you."

"It flows like water in my hand." He said. The reddish glow washed over his face. "Cuts like light through darkness."

"It's a bit small for a big guy like you, isn't it?" He knew I was complimenting him just like in the old days. He'd get a question right and I'd act shocked. He'd beat me in a race and I'd tell him it was only because his Mystis was empty.

"It's perfect." He said. "Absolutely perfect."

I stifled a laugh because I had said the same thing to Nurmedov about Daisey.

It showed how different Ilan and I had become.

Nomyds swore never to lift a sword. Instead, it would be within. My sword was in my Mystis and his was in his hand.

His sword looked a lot sharper than mine.

He sheathed his sword and was about to say something as Nurmedov strode up, arms full of hot piroshki and sweet rolls in a heavy basket. My favorites were the chewy ones, long as a forearm and woven like knots.

"Eh, who's this lunk of tin?" Nurmedov called behind a pile of golden brown dough. "Did some fountain come to life? Did you touch one of the statues from the rock garden with your..." I stepped in front of him and stopped him from saying anything having to do with the words *Coven* or *Craft*.

Ilan was a Paladyr by the way. I had just seen his sword. He'd earned it in blood.

And it was very sharp. It cut like what?
Like light through darkness.

"He's a…" I went to say, but Ilan jutted his chin and stepped forward.

"Citizen, are you with her?" Ilan bristled, acting all protective, which I found very endearing.

"With her? What do you mean *with* her?"

"What do you mean what do I mean?"

"You know what I mean, tin man, and my name's not *citizen*."

I could nearly hear them growl and bark and rolled my eyes. If they had tails, they could be wild dogs. If they had tails and wings, they could be dragons. I half expected them to drop everything and grapple right there in the town square for no good reason.

I came between them.

"Nurmedov, this is Il…er…um…Paladyr. Of The Infernium."

Nurmedov only squinted, which didn't suit him. I was sure he was quite tough, being an adventurer and all. He'd probably scaled the white mountains and seen winter Wights face to face to prove if the legends of the caves were truth. But he sure didn't look tough or intimidating next to broad-shouldered Ilan and his silver armor and emerald cape, and Nurmedov's attempt to stare down the much taller and powerfully built Paladyr was farcical.

Nurmedov grumbled a greeting.

"Paladyr, this is Nurmedov. He is a…"

"Traveller." Nurmedov added.

"Yes, a traveller who is accompanying me to…"

"Perisaris."

"Right," I nodded, knowing that Perisaris was *not* across the sea and there'd be no need for our expensive dragon purchases.

Or the mountainous basket of piroshki Nurmedov was hugging close to himself as if his life depended on it.

Ilan only nodded, sharply, and the two men stared at each other for a few tense moments before Nurmedov broke out in laughter so hard veins popped out in the middle of his forehead.

I can't believe that I hadn't gathered until that moment that it'd all been an act for Nurmedov. He'd been pushing Ilan's buttons all too easily. What a rogue...

He set down the basket and leaned against me as his body heaved with laughter, which confused Ilan even more.

"Oh, you young buck..." Nurmedov wiped his eyes. "So full of the Law."

"Excuse me?" Ilan said.

"Take it easy, man." Nurmedov slapped his shoulder and stood close. "I'm just playing with you. It's too easy for a guy like me. Nothing's serious, you know. Nothing ever will be. Life's just an adventure. Can't live it standing still."

Nurmedov pinched Ilan's ear which caused Ilan to jump and stare in bewilderment as Nurmedov hitched the basket of bread and baked goods over his shoulder, threw me a wink, and walked off down the square to where our dragons were waiting near the market.

"Is he..." Ilan trailed off.

Is he crazy?

"Very much." I said, my eyes swelling. "*Very* much."

"He is?"

"Yes. He's...umm...incurable."

"How'd you fall in with him?" Ilan asked, settling down in his stance.

But two trumpet blasts pricked both of our ears and his suntanned face paled. His spine straightened.

"Something's happened." He said, hand falling to his sword. "Wait here, okay? I'll be right back."

I smiled and watched him run off through the near empty square the opposite the way Nurmedov had gone and I ground my teeth at what my Sanctus was telling me the trumpet blasts were for.

I did not wait for Ilan.

THIRTEEN

I was in a run by the time I left the square and the world went black for a moment as strong hands grabbed me and pulled me into the shadows.

It was Nurmedov, his nostrils flared.

"Are you crazy? What the Hex are you thinking?"

"What?"

"Chatting up a Paladyr!" He threw a sarcastic eye to Xander. "She must be *really* good, X. So good she can't tell the difference between bravery and madness."

Like Nurmedov would know the difference.

Xander stood tall in the near perfect dark of the alleyway, looking stern and impossible to please.

"He used to be my best friend!"

Hands on his hips, Nurmedov moved his jaw left and right as if it was his unhinged scales of justice. He didn't know what to think about me and finally said,

"The truth."

"I told you. We were friends. We went to school together. At Bayh."

"No no no. About *you.*"

"About me?" I squeaked.

Then I swallowed.

My eyes flicked over to Xander, who may as well have been made of stone.

"Yeah, *you.*" Nurmedov said. "What are you?"

"I'm a..."

"If you say anything other than the truth we're both leaving."

His words cut me. Again, I looked to Xander for help, but he said nothing.

"You can't do that." I said.

"I sure can. I may be crazy, but I'm not stupid. Whereas you..."

My face flushed and I took a step back. He could've said anything else and it wouldn't have hurt as much.

He could've said anything but the truth.

But he'd said the truth. Stupid was what I was. What I couldn't get around. What I couldn't leave behind forever no matter how hard I tried. Whenever I went to feel something and live in the moment, my Mystis would cage me in and hold me down. Muzzle me.

Still the knowing. Smother it.

Kill it.

I said nothing, my hands slowly balling into fists. That didn't stop Nurmedov.

"I'm sure that strapping young oak tree of a man would just *love* to give you a tour of The Infernium. The barracks where they train stone cold killers. The mess halls where they eat human bones and share their many stories of ripping CovenCrafters from their homes late at night and burning them alive. The cells, deep underground, where vile creatures you didn't even know exist torture prisoners day and night. Night and day."

"Nurmedov...stop it." I warned him. I was shaking. Shaking to think Ilan would do that.

Ilan, the boy could tickle small fishes from the creek to show me how pretty they were, in the sunlight, only to set them back in the creek as if they were made of glass.

Nurmedov didn't stop.

"Especially if you ask to see his runesword again. If he knew you were the one who killed the Zerbrys he'd get a commendation for taking off your head and giving it to his commanders in a basket. But wait, you *didn't* kill that Zerbrys, did you?"

I opened my mouth and nothing came out.

The trumpets blasted twice again, far off, and Nurmedov pressed his gaze once to Xander and then stormed away.

Xander stared at me. Through me.

Still, I didn't know what to say.

A nearly imperceptible emotion stretched across his thin and needle-like features.

And then he uncrossed his arms and turned his back on me. Walking away.

"Stop." I said, weakly. Tears welled in my eyes. "Stop!"

My voice throbbed. Why did everyone always leave me?

"Stop!"

He didn't. His long stride took him from me breath by breath.

"Stop!"

The alley would end soon. Darkness would swallow him up. He'd be gone forever.

"I know how I woke you up!" I shouted.

He stopped.

I felt like it was the top of my lungs but it was just a peep. The voice of a mouse.

I watched his head bow and he turned, to squint at me over his shoulder. Silently, he beckoned me.

Show me. The doubt in his eyes said. *Make me believe.*

I sucked up all my sorrow and wiped the wetness from my face.

Ten strides placed us eye to eye. I reached out my hand, fingers splayed, and closed my eyes for a moment to dive deep within that imperfectly pure desire to heal the hurting and broken and make this world a better place.

And then I opened my eyes and touched his forehead.

If light had a feeling, I felt it. If the color of the sun at its peak could be compressed, like paper folded over itself again and again and again and again and placed in my palm, then it sure as snow had been.

In my hand. On his head. In his head.

My eyes were the size of Kalazaris itself as Xander shivered and fell in a heap at my feet.

I stared at him, shocked.

The trumpets blasted again, shaking me loose. Stars above, they were close. Just beyond the square. Behind us.

Nurmedov popped into my vision from the far edge of the alley. His honeywood bow was on his back, as was his heavy pack. The four bejeweled daggers caught a twinkle of light leftover from whatever I had done.

"What the Hex!" He ran forward. "What...?"

"I..." I stammered. "I only touched him!"

Nurmedov slowed and looked at me with awe and then back at Xander. All the awe left. Misunderstanding and impatience took over.

"You blasted Crafters..." He said, picking lanky Xander up and hoisting him over his shoulder as if he were a sack of grain. "I hate all of you! We'll talk about this later!" He called out as he turned and broke into a run, with Xander's limp arms flapping in the breeze.

I wanted to ask why but I didn't have to.

The thunderous footsteps of Paladyrs flooded the square.

Crunch crunch crunch crunch.

I took off, as fast as I could, following Nurmedov to where our dragons were waiting. Where we were off to, I didn't know. I didn't care. I just knew I couldn't have my life turned upside down in a matter of moments and hang around to let The Infernium help me make sense of it all.

They only knew *one* way to deal with CovenCrafters and there was no doubt in my mind Ilan was amongst them.

But we were friends, right?

Once...

Didn't that count for something?

Once friends or not, there was no way I wanted to be on the other side of that sword of his when it was drawn.

It was hungry and red and covered with runes that begged for CovenCrafter blood.

For my blood.

FOURTEEN

Our dragons awaited, heavy packs and all, in a covered section of the market that had been abandoned due to an outbreak of snow fleas.

I figured every little prickling sensation I felt was sweat and swiftness, and didn't stop to think about the little creatures hopping all over me.

All I could think about were the thunderous steps of The Infernium. My skin crawled but my ears were stretched so far to feel how many there were. Where they were marching. Their tactics. Their hunger for glory.

Especially since I already knew who they were after.

Nurmedov had all but thrown Xander on top of the dragon he'd purchased for the CovenCrafter and I marveled at his physical strength. The larger Xander was a paper doll in his arms. I blushed at the curses Nurmedov mumbled in hoisting him to the saddle. Xander's dragon, Nilius, who looked like a shaggy curly-haired snowball tree with long legs and a blunt little black nose, sat through the whole ordeal patiently.

"Come on already!" He shouted at me, strapping Xander into the saddle and securing the heavy packs. Nilius was the largest of the dragons by far, but his movements were silent, his dark eyes distant. Save his pale and shaggy hair, it was as if he wasn't even there. He was a fluffy statue.

I passed beneath Bailey's long muzzle. He was the rangy Komoridonian Nurmedov had chosen for himself. His fur was striped and swirled in black and brown, warm with a reddish hue. He flashed me a vampire's snarl of a smile and I shuddered as the thunder came closer. He was jittery in the excitement, pacing in a circle. He licked my neck as I passed and the touch of his cold tongue made me aware of the other sensations on my skin that had nothing to do with The Infernium.

Yes, there were fleas in my clothes.

I brushed at them as I ran over to Daisey. She was sleeping soundly on her side, wide pink tongue hanging out on the ground as her fat belly heaved like the bellows of a smithy. I'd heard sawteeth in tree bark at the hands of youth that sounded quieter than her snoring.

"Daisey, wake up!" I shouted, nearly out of breath. "Daisey!"

A small whimper passed through her body, and another, as a cloud of toxic breath hit me square in the face.

I winced. Fleas were crawling on me. Jumping over my arms, shoulders, on top of my head. I swatted them away. Daisey whimpered again, her eyes squeezed shut.

"She's dreaming! " Nurmedov said, rushing by on Bailey's back. "You have to wake her up!"

Bailey was ready to take off running and flap his broad wings to test the cold, clear skies. Nilius followed a pace behind, small eyes staring into the darkness of the winding alleys we'd run through.

Perhaps, like his master, he could see through walls, too.

While my dragon dreamt.

I scratched my head like a dog. I might've even growled. Fleas. So many of them I could barely breathe. They were everywhere. Thanks, Nurmedov. The Infernium was on their way to spit-roast me over hot coals and I was being eaten alive by snow fleas. Leaping around like little white spit peas in a skillet or drops of hail.

Gyyds above...

"Daisey!" I shouted. "Daisey girl!"

The dragon sat up with something that sounded like *huuumppph.* She looked around, hazily. Her long, gray beard was smushed and flattened across her long snout.

"Come on..." I said, as she grunted once more and let me on her back. Riding her was strange because she moved so slow and my heart beat so fast. I wanted to be in the air but we couldn't. I wanted to be gone from Kalazaris in a flash of light but we had to walk, single file, through the abandoned section of the market and another zigzag of alleys to get to another square. A bigger one, where we could make a run for the skies, and then the sea.

I clenched my teeth and looked behind my shoulder. Still nothing. Nothing but nothing itself, dead and dormant. Stagnant. Still. If so, then why didn't my heart slow down any? Why didn't the thunder rolling through the streets stop its *clomp clomp clomping*? Why did the footsteps sound like they were everywhere, and not just behind us? Like a fortress had been emptied.

I squinted and still, I could see nothing. Even with the red sun reaching higher and higher, Kalazaris was a carved-up cavern of clay and stone, bricks and pyramid-topped buildings. It'd been built upon over and over again, like a bandage on a wound. Open spaces were hard to find. Most of Kalazaris never saw the sun. Darkness dwelt and roamed wherever it pleased. It was an ancient place, and we were lost in its bowels. I told myself I would have to be brave if I wanted to live to see the beautiful light of the orange sun. High above it all. Sailing on the back of my dragon straight into the sea. Not stuck down here with the damned fleas and the quick promise of an Infernium prison cell.

Daisey grunted and shuddered beneath me. I wasn't heavy, but she was old, and she was getting used to carrying the weight. Apparently her own weight was burden enough. Nurmedov had strapped a few packs on her body before she slept, but in comparison to the other dragons they were the weight of feathers.

I stretched up in the saddle to see where we were going, but could only see the outline of Nurmedov's honeywood bow in the shadows, and the careful unfurling of Bailey's brown wings. Reaching out to scrape the walls that shrunk around us as we knifed through the alleys. It was as if he was pushing against the cramped alley. Fighting it. Keeping it away from Nurmedov.

I told myself to calm down. I told myself it would be okay. Even as the walls of the alley narrowed around me and my pulse fluttered in my ear like sea tide, I told myself I would make it out alive. That we would *all* see the sky. That no Infernium steel would split us open.

But as one alley ended and another began, I threw a glance over my shoulder.

Ilan.

He was a flash of silver and red. His emerald cape was jewel green water and wind. Fluid and swift and deadly. He was running toward us as fast as he could. His sword was drawn.

And he was not alone.

FIFTEEN

Nurmedov saw the Paladyrs closing in, and when I turned back to the alley to spur Daisey forward, he was nearly out of sight. Something kicked in Daisey without my having anything to do with it, and she nearly threw me as she took off after the fleeing dragons.

It took all I had to hold on.

My eyes misted in the wind. I didn't even bother to look back for fear of losing my balance. We were literally flying through the alleys. Ears and wings pinned back like sleek statues, body low and stretched to eat up the ground, we were really flying. Only on all fours.

It was magical and it nearly made me sick. The alleys twisted and dipped, connecting to one another in unnatural angles. Some were cut by low overhangs of clay blocks where dwellings jutted into the causeway. Several more were draped with recently cleaned clothes and carpets. There were times when I thought this giant square of our escape would just appear out of nowhere but no. Darkness streaked into more darkness. Dizzying and never ending. I wondered if Nilius knew the layout of Kalazaris like Xander did. If they had some sort of Mystis-sharing going on. I couldn't say no to these ideas anymore. If a knowing rose up, I would not cast it down, and that's what rose up. I even stretched once to see if Xander was awake and guiding Nilius but I got thwapped in the face by a pair of damp breeches that blinded me for a moment till the wind of our momentum tore them away. The sting of them left a red mark on my forehead and reminded me to stop thinking and hold on tight. But with our zigzagging path, I figured we had diverted our intended direction at least ten times over. My sense of direction was lost to nausea with our swiftness. And the dragons? They were immune to the peril. It was but a game to them and their lightning quick feet. Bailey was chasing Nilius. Daisey was chasing Bailey. And The Infernium couldn't catch fat old Daisey even if they were on horseback. She still had enough magic in her tubby body to keep me alive, and holding on to her as she shot through the city made all the peril of being caught disappear. The only peril left was to hang on. In wider alleyways, their furry wings would stretch and arc to keep their balance as they raced along the uneven cobblestones and I swear there were little streaks of white vapor kissing their wingtips.

When the square finally did open up before us, I was breathless and sore. Walking and riding were very different things.

The soreness in my lower back and legs flew up to my Mystis, and I groaned and covered my face in my hands.

Because, as the sky opened up broad and beautiful above the cold angles of the building tops, it was painfully obvious that the juicy orange midday sun was dimmed. Blurred.

Blocked.

The square was covered in a film. A milky white sheet that rippled above it. An invisible ceiling. Light washed through the milky film like a driven tide.

It was a barrier. Crafted. Crafted by whom?

I lowered my hands and stretched in the saddle as the dragons slowed and took to the near edge of the empty square.

Sure enough, there was a lone figure at the other end of the square.

I wanted to curse at whatever was about to happen. It may've been over my head, but it sure was giving me a headache.

The square was giant. Ringed by stoic building blocks and their pyramid tops. By statues and fountains and places to sit.

And no people.

Yes, I looked up to the barrier again. It was alive. Swirling with energy. I stared at the barrier and then at the lone figure across the empty space.

The setting had been prepared. Carefully planned.

It was a trap.

We'd been funneled into a trap.

And that sick feeling I'd fought when lurching around the alleys in a blurry haze fell down to my guts.

Because the *clomp clomp clomp* of The Infernium trickled around the edge of my ears like a distant thunderstorm.

We'd distanced ourselves from them, but we hadn't lost them. We *couldn't* lose them. Not till we took to the skies and flew across the sea.

I wondered why that's all I wanted. I didn't know Xander and he didn't know me, save the moments when I had touched him with my hands, and when he had touched me with his words.

Why was I already in so deep with these two guys and our dragons? I still didn't know where we were going or what Xander and Nurmedov were seeking across the sea. I was about to leave everything behind and I could think about nothing else but the incredible need to do so. I wanted to put a sea between me and my fifteen years of life. Between me and this city.

Between me and Ilan.

But my breath left me as the lone figure across the square advanced slowly. With heavy purpose.

Because Xander slid from Nilius' saddle and strode forward with a lazy swagger. He rolled his neck so that the bones popped and cracked. He squeezed his hands to fists and snorted a deep breath of air. Then threw me a look that stilled my heart.

The knowing within that moment was a cruel thing. A silent knife cutting deep.

For within Xander's hard black eyes slept immense darkness. Roaring and swirling and churning and burning.

Awake and alive way down within his stone cold Tempus like an open wound that could never heal.

And to save us, this day, he would dive deep within that wound to touch its power.

To unleash it.

The thunderous steps rattled closer. Munching up the lost distance like hungry teeth to a feast. They must've emptied every garrison in Kalazaris to find us.

But what did that matter?

The silent steps of the lone figure across the square scared the snot out of me. And I wiped my nose on my sleeve as Xander swallowed and walked forward, leaving us behind.

I heard his black leathers croaking. Hard-soled boots smacking the cobblestones. A small wind brushed his ermine cloak. His slick black hair and needle-like features were dead set on death itself.

He was ready to die so that we could live.

I hated that thought, and threw myself from Daisey's back.

It didn't matter how close the Paladyr's were or were not as long as that barrier was above us.

And I had gifts within me. A secret language. I had Craft if only I followed it. If only I told my Mystis and all that I thought I knew to shut up and leave me alone. If only I stood by Xander's side and trusted him.

I ran forward and fell in step with him. He slowly turned to behold me and fought a frown.

I reached out and took his hand in mine. To touch him. A faint flicker washed across his face as my hand burned to hold his. His was so cold. So cold. I held it tighter and tried to imbue to him what I had when I had knocked him out. It was still far too much to process, but I had no time to stop and think. I had acted then, I was acting now. I squeezed his hand as tight as I could and swallowed the nausea that told me I was going to be blasted into a million pieces by the figure across the square.

For even my Mystis knew the lone figure was a CovenCrafter. And the only knowing I had on the subject was dread. Pure dread.

The need for a duel sat in the air, tense and static. Some unresolved issue crawling out into the light of day. We had finally come to the end of the road in Kalazaris, only to find it was conflict.

And to whatever end, Xander and I were in it together.

SIXTEEN

The voice came to us as if from the other side of a chasm, though nothing separated us.

"Do you remember me, son of night and shadow?"

It was a woman's voice. Hoarse and strangled.

Ancient.

Not old, though...a young voice from years ago. Lost, somehow. A life stolen. A hollow reflection of a once vibrant Sanctus swirling in a stormwind.

"Well, do you?"

Xander's chin tipped up, his eyes harder than ever. He strained to hold back his anger. Whatever sat between them was raw and alive.

"How can I forget?"

"Who is she?" I whispered.

"I never knew her name." He said. "But she is a Pryystys of Thanem."

Thanem, Gyyd of the Woven Worlds. With the void for a face, a cloak of stars and space, and Gyyds for hands, to invoke Thanem was to invoke the highest authority there was.

If one believed in all that.

"Is she...?"

"Dangerous?" Xander grimaced. "Very."

"But we can take her, right?"

"Take her?" Xander arched me an eyebrow. "Rosalyn, what happened when I...*took* that Zerbrys?"

"I passed out."

Xander grimaced again.

"This Pryystys is no Zerbrys. You could line up a hundred of those three headed beasts and she'd flatten them with the flick of her wrist."

"That bad?"

"And that barrier above us? She's blocked off the wind. The weather. It means all my environmental work is limited. I'll have to work or weave with what we have here."

"No blizzard?"

"No, Rosalyn." He looked around. "But I'll think of something."

I bit my lip.

"Leave the girl behind and face me alone." The woman intoned. She was closer now. Death was in her voice. A tremor rushed up my spine. "I hold no qualm with her. But you, son of night and shadow, you bind me to my death oath."

"I'm with him!" I shouted before Xander could say anything. Before I could process the gravity of the phrase *death oath.*

The cloaked figure may've looked at me, because I shivered. I couldn't see her face. Like the altars of Thanem, the face was hidden in a heavy hood, so that the void itself was all I could see.

"You know not of his crimes, girl."

"And you know not of his..." I shouted, pausing because I didn't know what the opposite of *crime* would've been. Oops. I might as well have stuck my foot in my mouth and crossed my eyes. I was trying to tell her he was a good guy and I wasn't going to bail out just because she showed up.

Xander stepped forward with a stilling hand between us.

"Say no more." He said. "Let us settle this."

"I'll settle this." Nurmedov said. I hadn't heard him sneak up behind us. His bow was off his back with an arrow notched in it before I could blink my eyes.

The arrow whistled toward the woman and she raised her hands to mirror Thanem's stone effigies. Flames rose in her hands and what was once an arrow became a pile of ash at her feet as it passed through the flames.

Nurmedov's mouth sagged open.

"That arrow was warded..." He said in disbelief.

"By whom?" Xander smirked.

"By matrons of the sun cult."

"Better go get your money back."

I looked back at the woman and the flames fizzled out in her hand. She looked down at the ash and bent down to work it.

There was a lump in my throat. I'd seen Xander work wind and snow and his own breath to make a sword of ice. I hated to think of what she was doing with that ash.

"Go get the dragons ready to fly." Xander told Nurmedov. "Make sure they don't spook." Xander turned his eyes once again to the Pryystys as she moved her hands across the pile of ash. "This is going to get messy."

Xander squeezed my hand. I looked down at it, startled. I had forgotten.

"Whatever happens, don't let go of my hand." He said. "We're going to do this together."

I searched his face. His hard eyes, his narrow features. Sunken cheeks. The black slick of his hair and the perfect cleanliness of his regal clothes.

He squeezed my hand again.

"I need you." He said, his voice low. "You called me back from the hopeless abyss."

Surprise leaked across my face.

"I..."

I didn't know what to say.

"I'll make sense of everything when we get out of here, okay? Just don't let go. No matter what. *Don't* let go."

I nodded and swallowed my fears.

And turning back to the Pryystys, they were rekindled once again.

In one hand she held a large round shield with a heavy boss. Runes were etched into the shield like a cryptic puzzle. The shield looked rough and flaky, the color of ash.

The other hand was low at her side as she walked forward.

Her fingertips were soaked in flames.

SEVENTEEN

My Mystis told me ash cannot burn. So she was stealing Xander's chance to fight fire with fire. And like he'd said, no blizzard.

What else did that leave?

I didn't know much about CovenCraft, but I knew fire and ice were their own forms of Gyyds. Little could stand against them.

Xander didn't give me a chance to think as he pulled me behind him and stretched out his arm at his side, fingers splayed.

"Back up." He said, and I backed up as we gave ground to the Pryystys, who was in no rush. I peeked a look past Xander's elbow and watched as she twisted the shield back and forth. It looked like it was spinning. The runes were blurring together.

It was hypnotic.

"Don't look." He said.

I squeezed my eyes shut.

"And what you did back there in the alley...what you did on the highway? I need all of it, Rosalyn. All you have."

I looked down at our hands. Even the passing of cobblestones beneath our feet made me motion sick. But his hand? His cold, cold hand? I could hold onto that. I could do that.

There was a great grinding sound to our left and my mouth sagged as one of the statues jerked from its pedestal and fell to the ground. Bits of marble broke off in chunks. Coughs of dust shrouded the statue. It was like there was a rope that held it fast and Xander had pulled it.

Still the Pryystys advanced.

And the air around us cooled.

I squeezed Xander's hand and it burned. It burned because his body was as cold as ice.

Xander slapped his hand across her image. She flinched and lifted her shield as a white wave of frost sliced toward her. The arc hit the edge of her shield with the crisp sound of crackling leaves. Xander's attack bleached her shield somewhat. No damage.

The Pryystys took a hop step and lunged. Nearly flat on the ground, her attack was sleek and refined. She blew on her hand and a jet of fire flashed our way.

Xander hugged me in his arms and the world spun as we rolled across the ground. The air where we had been was charred.

I looked on in disbelief. Black particles danced around like snow.

She had cooked the air.

"Xander..." I squeaked.

"No!" He roared as he pulled me up and held me close, my chest to his. My head buried in his shoulder. I couldn't see her but I could *feel* her advance. Even if I closed my eyes I could see her sway closer. Leonine and graceful.

"Let her go." The Pryystys said.

"No."

"If you truly cared for her you would."

The knowing hit me before the words hit the air and I sighed and buried my head in his shoulder.

"I don't care for her. She is here to give me more power."

The Pryystys laughed. Still I did not remove my hand from his.

The air shrieked as fire met ice. Xander's jagged arc of frost hissed and melted as Thanem's holy fire consumed whatever Xander called on for power. Maybe it was his own. His own cold blood in his veins. That's why he needed me.

I closed my eyes as he threw his hand out again. His ice hit her fire and she advanced with her shield. The air was too hot for it to do anything. It splashed on the ash. Hot water and steam. Soaking it. Beads of water flew from the shield as she spun it back and forth with those hypnotic runes.

I lifted my gaze and met Xander's. He frowned at me in that heartbeat of a moment and I didn't give him a chance to answer.

I pushed from him as if I was diving away from a cliff. Down, down, down into the raging ocean. I pushed away from Xander and ran into the hanging cloud of steam just as the Pryystys stepped from it, shield low in front of her belly, fire hand high above her head.

My presence froze her better than Xander's ice ever could. She straightened in shock but it was too late.

I leapt at her, madly, stretching my hands out to get her.

To touch her.

Our bodies collided with a thud. The mess was disorienting. We rolled, bodies entangled. I felt the ash shield smack against my left knee once and felt it no more. It was as hard as it was light. Like a razor of flaky rocks. The world righted itself and wobbled as the cobblestones greeted our backs like fists. A moan stretched from my mouth.

And then she was on me.

The hand that held the shield was pressed on my heart as she straddled me and crushed me to the cobblestones. Her hand of fire was raised, ready to fall.

The collision had stripped her of her hood. The hood that'd given her the face of the Gyyd she served. The void. And the face of flesh and bone that stared down at me was cruel and beautiful, young and doe-eyed.

As hot and hungry as Xander was cold and distant.

"I was trying to spare you, child!" She shouted.

"And I'm trying to stop you from killing him!" I managed.

Somehow, even more rage tore through that dead voice of hers. That hollowed howl. It jellied my spine.

"Who are you to meddle with the fate of Ozmander?" She shouted. "Who are you to meddle with destiny?" I squinted at her anger, as if I was being blasted in the face by the hot air of an oven. "You will die for what you have done!"

But it was only my Mystis that died in that moment. Never to recover.

The knowing that flooded me covered me inside and out like the barrier that blocked our escape. A wash of tide. It was liquid, like blood or water, but it was thick and gluey, like syrup.

It was as if a vessel locked within had been broken. A clay pot cracked. And I could not stop the spill.

I screamed and reached for that cruel and beautiful face with both hands just as her grip of fire fell straight down for my neck.

EIGHTEEN

A flash of light, a compressed cushion of sunshine, flared across her body as all ten fingertips framed her face.

For one moment, her gaze was a fallen star. Streaking through the sky. Exploding.

And the scream she tore from my throat was as hot and painful as her grip of fire. Her hand closed around me. Grasping for the flaming choke that would kill me.

But it was only a kiss. Her grip flew from my neck just as soon as it had touched it.

And I knew why.

The Pryystys staggered back. Her doe eyes were no longer brown, but blanched like boiled eggs. Her hands were out in front of her, slashing at the air.

She was blind.

I crab-crawled away from her as she staggered back. My breath was hard to catch. To see what'd happened in the blink of an eye. It was marvelous and frightening. But my Mystys had been shattered into a thousand pieces. All I had to hold onto was the broken vessel of knowing.

Of a Sanctus awakened. Spilling within me. Seeping into every corner of who I was.

For the searing pain at my throat was meaningless in comparison to the images that invaded my Mystis as I had touched her. Fractured, like bits of pottery. Rippling like rain on a lake.

I turned back to Xander who stood perfectly still, chest heaving in the slightest.

Shame was awash on his face.

He knew that I knew. He knew that I had seen it all.

"Who are you?" I whispered.

He only shook his head. The hardness in his eyes spoke words I could not understand.

The images were of the Temple of Thanem, so long ago. A blood-soaked scene where the High Pryystys had offered up two children to be burned in Thanem's open palms.

Two children. Whose children?

Twin sons of the dark lord Ozmander, and their mother, the High Pryystys of Thanem.

I shivered.

A Paladyr had saved them. *A Paladyr? Really? A Paladyr?*

Yes, a Paladyr. One as fearless as a winter Wight. He'd burned the High Pryystys in her own sacrificial fire and killed all of her acolytes with the sword and a blur of masterful TempusCraft.

All but one.

Xander drew in shallow breaths, his thin lips pressed in a line.

I repeated myself to no avail.

"Who *are* you?"

He looked past me. Behind me, the Pryystys stumbled. Her world had gone dark. She fell to the ground with something of a choking sound. Stripped of her shield. Robbed of her sight.

I watched as she mumbled something, filled with sorrow, and a reddish doorframe appeared in the air before her as if traced by two fingers. She lunged for it and fell in awkwardly as it disappeared, and she with it.

As if she were never there.

A sucking noise tore my gaze from Xander up to the sky. The barrier flew with her, as if attached to her.

I staggered back. It was all too much.

All of it.

Xander's words...what he'd said, what he wouldn't say. A fight with a Pryystys of Thanem that made me literally lose my Mystis.

And the bloodstains of a dark history. Now locked in the hollows of my head.

It was too much.

Xander approached as I walked around in a daze. I was trying to think...trying to stitch the pieces together like always. Trying to add words and numbers together. Logic. Reason. Memory.

They were all gone.

All that responded to me was the knowing of my Sanctus.

And the raw power of the high sun that sloshed within like sea tide.

I wanted to be sick. Sickness fizzled along my skin, clammy and unsure. Maybe I could release it all. Throw it up. Then I'd be back to normal.

Nope. There was no normal. Never again.

I could not unsee what I had seen. I could not close what had been opened up.

I could not forget what Xander had said.

The CovenCrafter's hands were on me. I tore myself away from them.

Again, they sought to shackle me. To calm me. Contain me.

"No!" I shrieked, trying to turn away. Trying to give myself a moment to think and sort it all out...only to *know* that I couldn't.

That I didn't even know how anymore.

Xander tried to reach for me again and I pushed past him and began to run.

Only to stop in my tracks.

Surrounding Nurmedov and our furry dragons were the silver teeth of The Infernium, glazed in the orange juice of the high noon sun.

They were living statues at the ready. Their weapons were sheathed, but their faces were grim for war.

Their leader walked towards us, his steps heavy, hand on his sword.

It was Ilan.

He'd seen it all. I knew it.

I *knew* it.

And at this distance I couldn't quite see his face but I could read his expression.

Disappointed.

At what I'd become? At what *he'd* become? At what would finally separate us for good and drive coffin nails into the day when I cried on his shoulder?

I walked forward and leaned low to pick up the ash rune shield and fit it to my left arm.

I wasn't going to take the chance.

NINETEEN

The Infernium Soldyrs behind Ilan tensed with my every step. They'd seen the light. They were afraid of me. Afraid of what they didn't know.

"Rosalyn..." Ilan warned, his hand flat toward me. What was I, a wild beast? A specter of the celestial? A creature of the deep?

I stopped, bouncing on my feet. Jaw set. I was mad. Seething mad. I wanted to smash my palm into the cobblestones and blast this little square into the mountains. I wanted to send all of my problems far away from here.

Even though I knew I could not.

SanctusCraft did not work that way. It was not raw emotion. It was not the raging fire of an avenging Pryystys, or the cold manipulation of an enigmatic mystic.

But, for the life of me, I could not understand why Ilan, of all people, had to stand in the way of this moment? Of this heartbeat when my life had forever changed and left me to stagger around the aftermath.

If any other square jaw sat above silver plate armor I would've...I would've...I don't know. Something. Something other than just staring and waiting for him to make a move that told me he still cared about me as a person and didn't see me as a monster. As a freak that I didn't even know that I was. Couldn't he see beyond that? Beyond the creed that said he as a Paladyr had to hunt and kill CovenCrafters? Could I explain to him in but a moment what it felt like? How

liberated I was? How, as strange as it all was, I never wanted
to go back to the burden that being myself had been to me!
Could he know that? Could he just *know* that in a heartbeat
as I knew the things that I knew now?

Xander had told me it would be easy. Another veiled
falsehood. Knowing was easy. The repercussions of it were
not.

"Rosalyn..." Ilan said again.

"What?"

"Think about this."

"Think about what?"

"You don't want to do this."

"Do what?"

His eyes jerked to the shield. Still, he hadn't drawn his
sword.

I pointed behind him, behind our fuzzy dragons and
the clouds of their breath as they panted, tongues wagging in
the breeze. With so many Soldyrs behind them, I thought of
their safety. I didn't want such sweet creatures to get hurt.

"Call your men off and maybe we'll talk."

His inhale was sharp. His chin nicked to the left and
then slowly to the right. As if to say, *I would if I could, Rosy.*

But I can't change. Not even for you.

*I'm a Paladyr now. I kill CovenCrafters. No matter who
they are.*

No matter who they were.

He took a step closer, gently. As if I was going to bolt.
Or scream a warcry.

I only stared at him, trying to see through him.

Everything good about him, everything I remembered,
had been lost in that moment when my Sanctus had broken
free and taken me over. When the knowing had shown me
SanctusCraft and its power.

And the river eyes that stared back at me whispered
something else. Not something about the past I didn't
remember. But something about the future that I shouldn't
be so quick to judge.

I hefted the shield and crouched. Ilan stopped.

In that moment, I didn't know. I didn't *know.*

And it was because of Xander's words. How they conflicted with everything else he'd said.

Conflicted?

Complimented.

I need you. You called me back from the hopeless abyss...

And what you did back there in the alley...what you did on the highway? I need all of it, Rosalyn. All you have...

I don't care for her. She is here to give me more power...

I didn't want to deal with Ilan because I needed to deal with Xander.

We had a lot to talk about.

"Rosalyn, please." Ilan's pleading shook me from thought. "Make this easy for me."

I frowned at him. He was closer. His stride was stretched. Still sneaking up on me.

"Would you kill me?" I said. "Does your creed mean that much to you?"

"Creed?" Ilan straightened. "You're a Nomyd! You took an oath!"

I heard a moan from Nurmedov who flipped a half eaten piroshok over his back shoulder and dropped his head into his hands.

A Nomyd.

A wanderer bound to help or heal. Never to hurt. Never to harm.

A celibate. A student. A stray cat with no true home.

"You're a Nomyd." Ilan said again, softer, as if that was the bridge to bring me closer to him and an underground cell.

"Am I?" I asked, wide eyed at the thought. "Am I the product of those who threw me out to the wolves? Am I the mouthpiece of their useless knowledge when knowledge itself hums inside my heart for *once* in my life? Am I what you think I am? Am I what you remember? Who you remember? Who you *think* you used to know?"

Was I talking to him or myself?

"Rosalyn, don't. Don't think this...*magic* is any sort of truth. Don't you dare."

"And don't you dare tell me what I am to believe!" I roared, shaking at the power surging just beneath my skin. Ready to leap out at my touch. The silent roar of the sun as it burned a hole in the pale sky. Seething just beneath my skin. "You abandoned the Nomyd Creed for the blood-soaked path of The Infernium! Don't you dare tell me what my truth is when you have so radically changed your own! And abandoned those who loved you in the process..."

Ilan only swallowed. The air around him was frigid. Still. His breath came in a cloud.

After a heartbeat he spoke, his voice rough and dirty.

"Those who practice CovenCraft *must* be killed." He said. "And so I am bound."

Ilan drew his sword. The sun kissed it with warm fire. Light snaked down its runes, alive and ready to cleave my bones as if they were made of paper.

I grit my teeth.

"Ilan...would you slay me?"

Ilan winced, his nostrils flared. Emotion was hot in his blue eyes. A sea boiling because a sword of fire had been plunged deep inside.

"I AM BOUND!"

I screamed as he charged me, and threw the ash shield toward his tall frame and the swiftness in which he closed on me.

But it didn't matter.

An icy wind thrust its fingers into the square and yowled. Pushing and shoving. Dividing. The clatter of sword and shield and armor was a harmless rattle just on the edge of hearing. Moans and groans were lost in the rush of air. Bodies were thrown across the square. Flattened by invisible fists.

The dragons lurched and shot forward in a run, Nurmedov stretching to rein them all in.

"I'm sorry!" Xander shouted over the howl as he grabbed my arm.

Following him step for step was all I could do not to lose my footing. He pulled me forward, through the frosty chaos, till Nurmedov was upon us.

The spark of adventure was alive in his eye, not that it ever died, and Bailey reared on his hind legs before Nurmedov released a series of woops and spurred the dragon on into the wind. In a step and a half they were gone. Their shadow crossed our face until they cleared the pyramid tops of the dwellings edging the square.

Xander pushed me up onto Daisey's back. Her long gray beard fluttered in the wind, and she squinted through the frost.

"Come on, Daisey girl!" I shouted, and she set off in a slow walk, yawning.

Xander raised one arm and whipped it around his head as the wind changed direction.

Daisey but spread her furry black wings and the cold wind slipped under us like an unseen palm, lifting us up and up and up.

A smile stretched across my face. It was marvelous! The heaviness of knowing was silenced within me. Wonder filled its place. Elevation was like a drug. Lightening my head on my shoulders. Fresh air filled my lungs.

Until there was a tug on the saddle blanket. I turned around and saw nothing. Nothing but Kalazaris shrinking.

Daisey blinked lazily as she tipped a wing to follow Bailey, who was flapping wildly as Nurmedov spurred the dragon higher and higher into the cloudless sky, straight into the orange eye of the sun.

I felt the tug again and turned to see two hands straining to pull the body they belonged to up onto the dragon's back.

It was Ilan.

Xander pulled up alongside, sitting tall upon Nilius' puffy white back, the dragon coasting higher and higher.

A smile was on his face. A real smile.

Because Ilan was whiter than snow. The tall Paladyr was shaking and struggling to pull himself up in the saddle next to me like a drunk who'd fallen in a lake.

The lightness I'd so soon gained with our incredible escape was gone. And so was Xander, flying off ahead of me on Nilius' back. He was a fuzzy snowball thrown into the sky. Gone so quick I wondered if I'd imagined the smile on his face or if it had been just another one of those grimaces.

The wind tore at my hair as I looked behind me. Ilan hung on for dear life, shaking and gripping Daisey's fur so tight I feared he would rip it from her back.

I scoffed to myself and reached out my hand to touch him.

Ilan slept through the flight across the sea.

TWENTY

The night sun was violet when land finally appeared, just a string of sharp rocks breaking the flat line of the sea. White birds with long orange beaks perched on these rocks like military parade pennants, their caws and crows silent as they slept standing up. Past these giant fists poking through the sea, smaller rocks snaked around the foamy tide in small bridges of land, till all the rocky tendrils met at the shore.

We couldn't land at the shore. It looked like rows upon rows of jagged teeth. I was beginning to wonder where we were. Why we had come. Even though I knew we were where we wanted to be. Where we needed to be. A place where we could stop and slow down.

Where I could get the answers I needed.

Yes, I had *so* many questions for Xander, whom I no longer trusted.

Our dragons seemed to relax to see the land and smell it with their little wet noses, peering across the land as we followed the jagged black rocks until the sun ran red.

With the dawn of a new day came a small sense of relief. More of a hope that relief was in the future. Even with all my questions for Xander, and the fact that I'd have to deal with Ilan as he sat in direct opposition to our journey. And...well, he swung his sword at me. There was that small fact to address. To come to terms with.

Would Ilan kill me?

Would he kill Xander?

I still didn't know to what end our path lead, but I knew that Ilan was opposed to all things CovenCraft and we would have to face it. The knowledge that more CovenCraft lay ahead of us was unavoidable. Surely he'd know that as soon as he woke up.

Sleepy head.

Yes, Ilan would either have to follow along and witness the true power of CovenCraft and come to see its purpose, or, he would have to forever close himself off to it and continue seeing it as something to eradicate from the earth.

By death.

Just like The Infernium taught him.

But how easy was it for him to forget all that he'd learned behind the secluded walls of Bayh in order to adopt the ways of The Infernium? Or had he learned the ways of one in conflict to the other?

Speaking of conflict...

...while my struggles with Xander and Ilan made me heavy with doubt, seeing tufts of bleached sea grass poke up through the jagged rocks gave me hope. Across the sea, the sun looked less like blood and more like the juice of dark cherries. Salty sea air ruffled the bleached grass and I wanted to kick off my boots and let my hands snake through the stalks. I couldn't fight the thought. I was seeing a new land. It was exciting. I wanted to forget them both for a moment. Both of them and all my troubles.

I wanted to explore.

Following the shoreline for miles as it zigged and zagged reminded me of the twisted alleys of Kalazaris, and how following the shoreline to habitable land amidst the vast and endless sea to a place where we could land and settle down wasn't that much different than our flight from Kalazaris. To me, the gigantic sprawl of Kalazaris was a sea. Overwhelming. Filled with mysterious faces and swift currents. Voices. Confusion. Forces of nature. Death. I was glad to be free of its immensity. Its grandeur. And to cross the sea and come upon the land, I truly hoped that wherever we had come to would be a lot safer for us than Kalazaris had been.

So much had happened to me there. So many things I'd never forget. Things I was still in awe of.

Was it too much to ask for a moment to stop and sort it all out?

TWENTY-ONE

Bailey was frolicking along the shore when Xander found me.

We had landed on a grassy plain, easily sloping up and up until morning mist, colored pink by the red sun, stole the horizon from us. Behind me, the sea curled in a small cove where Bailey and Nurmedov were playing fetch with a piece of driftwood. Nurmedov was grinning ear to ear, hefting the wood as far out to sea as he could, watching the beast splash in after it, only to smile even broader once Bailey had the wood between his teeth to prance back onto shore and drop it at Nurmedov's feet.

The best part of it was Ilan. Still asleep, curled up next to a heap of saddlebags and packs, Nurmedov would talk to him. Tell him jokes only Nurmedov would find funny. Jokes about The Infernium and what sorts of morons would sign their life away to its sword and steel shackles. How an outfit that didn't allow women in its ranks was obviously flawed. How badly the food sucked in the mess hall. How he could escape their fabled cells with one hand tied behind his back.

Ilan, mouth open, would silently agree as his sleep made him nod and shiver.

Perhaps he was still dreaming of flight and how it scared the snot out of him.

Daisey, seemingly taken with the flavor of the grass, had wandered off to graze. Last thing I saw of her was her long and wise looking gray beard dancing in the wind. One of

Nurmedov's cherished sweet rolls was in my hand, a powdered one, but I didn't feel like eating it. Still, I took a bite as the pinkish mist seemed to part and allow Xander to swoop down the hill with his long stride. With his regal black leathers and princely cloak of ermine. With his dead expression.

I didn't want to look him in the eye. I felt sick to my stomach as he approached. Still I nibbled.

I hadn't seen him land. I had no idea where Nilius was. Lost in the pink mist, that lanky furry snowball. Probably up on the knoll that stood in front of us, staring down the length of the island to spy for Xander.

"Rosalyn..." He mumbled. "I feel that I owe you an explanation."

"You don't owe me anything." I said, bitterly. "You knew what you wanted. You knew what you were doing. You always do. Even if nobody else does."

He squinted at me. Studying me. His narrow features looked weather-worn and so much older than I remembered.

"What do you mean?"

"I figured it out." I said, taking a bite of the sweet roll. Staring at my fingers as the snow-like powder stuck to the swirls of my prints. "You provoked me somehow. You knew that if you could control the right environment it – meaning you could introduce controlled chaos...it would all come out. My SanctusCraft. My secret language. My touch."

His black eyes were on me, intently.

"You knew that whatever endowment of SanctusCraft I have would take me over." I continued. "But you lied by omission. You said that *knowing* was easy. You never said how hard it would be to live once you know."

There was a splash and the sound of laughter. Xander crossed his arms.

"It was a risk I had to take."

I sighed and threw the roll into the grass, looking him square in the eye.

And for once I was not afraid of the void that stared back.

"I don't trust you."

"Did you ever?"

"Yes." I nodded. "Yes I did." I bit back my anger. "And you ruined that."

"It was worth it." He said.

I opened my mouth but nothing came out. There was a knowing instead and I wanted to throw it farther out to sea than Nurmedov could throw the stick.

It was nearly impossible to say it.

But I did. An inch from his face, my finger in his chest. My skin red as the sun as he stood stoic and still.

"I provoked you? *Me*? You're blaming *me* for the fact that *you* used me? How…" I waved my hands around. "How is that even possible?"

He said nothing, but thumped my forehead with two fingers.

I took a step back.

This impossible, *impossible* man.

"So because…according to you, great mister…whatever you are, because there was some…dormant SanctusCraft in me, and my Mystis was too strong, you forced me to…what, loose my Mystis entirely??? Who said you could do that?"

Xander shook his head.

"Your Mystis isn't lost."

"Really? Then where the Hex is it?"

"It's just suppressed by the strength of your Sanctus."

"Great. Fun. Cool. Why does it feel like I've lost my Mystis forever?"

"It's not like that, Rosalyn."

"What's it like?" I shouted.

Nurmedov stopped throwing and fingered one of his daggers casually, his eyes dancing between both of us before looking back out to sea and throwing the driftwood. His lips moved to make a comment to Ilan that I could not hear. Ilan shifted uncomfortably and hugged himself tighter, his eyes squeezed shut. Nurmedov's laughter was lost in the wind.

"SanctusCraft is not a gift. It's not an ability or an endowment. It's a connection. There is the knowing and the touch. The work, weld, or weave depends on the situation. On the connection. The...interaction. Still, there is knowing, touch, and outcome. Simple as that. A connection unbroken."

I blinked and my mouth sealed itself. Something in his words soothed me, even though I told myself he was *not* to be trusted.

"You were nothing *but* your Mystis, Rosalyn. Your Mystis was your Gyyd. You had no connection to your Sanctus. To who you really are. To who you've always wanted to be." He ran a hand through the dark slick of his hair. "Your Mystis was merely a...cork in a wineskin. The lid on an endless well. All I did was force you to yank that cork out. To open that lid. But *you* started it. Not me. *You* were the catalyst. *You* were the reason."

"I was? How?"

"You started it when...when you touched me..."

"The first time?"

"Yes. On the road to Kalazaris. When you touched me..."

I frowned at the difficulty it brought him to even speak of it. As if a noose had been around his neck.

"...What did I do?"

"Like I said," he sighed. "You brought me back from the abyss."

Again I stared into his black eyes as he laid his hands on my shoulders and gripped them tight. His touch was cold, as if his own Sanctus was still as distant as it had seemed that first time we met. As if it had wandered outside of his body, outside of his Tempus.

I fought the knowing.

Was it possible? Could a Sanctus leave a Tempus and find its way back?

That was against every law of science I had been taught at Bayh. Only death could free the Sanctus from the Tempus...from skin and bone.

But the knowing...

Xander said I had *brought him back from the abyss*...and the more I thought about it, the more the chill of his touch seeped into me.

This time, I couldn't fight the dread sleeping in his gaze.

"That's why we're here, Rosalyn." He nearly whispered. "I have to go back."

"*You* have to go back?" My eyes swelled. A spray of sea wind made them tear. "To the abyss?"

He nodded. Again he was the broken man. Used up. Worn out. Resigned to a predestined fate. To doom.

The noose was still around his neck. Pulling taut. As if my touching him...and that *connection* between us was just a friendly reminder that the end was nigh but someone would hold his hand as the time came for him to pay for his crimes.

What crimes?

I knew everyone was after him for some reason but I couldn't bring myself to ask.

Not when the knowing of the moment was so obvious. Of why he needed me.

He actually *needed* me.

"And when you say *you* have to go," I continued, "you mean *we* have to go. To the abyss."

"That's right."

I spoke through the knowing. Now the doom that had been in his eyes was in my bones as well.

"You need me because I can bring you back from the abyss."

Again, he nodded, and the wind howled across the sea.

TWENTY-TWO

Daisey wandered back with red liquid dripping from her long gray beard. Nurmedov smiled at her and gathered some of it on his finger and tasted it. While that made me cringe, his words did the opposite.

"Ooh! Wild strawberries!"

Xander nodded, nostrils flared. I was surprised he could smell the sweet tang of wild strawberries over her nearly poisonous breath. I was thankful for the strong sea wind. I couldn't smell anything but cold salt and whitecaps.

"Leave it to the old girl to find something tasty on this desolate rock." Nurmedov hitched a stack of heavy packs. His own and Xander's. And while I wanted to think Xander was pompous enough in his princely clothes to act like he was above carrying supplies, I knew it was because he needed to be free to work, weave, or weld CovenCraft.

Because the need was always sitting there, hovering and brooding like the pulse of the earth.

The pink mist cloaking the rolling hills before us could hold a hundred horrors. A hundred thousand.

Or a patch of wild strawberries. Half-eaten.

Either way, we needed to be prepared. I didn't want to meet a Pryystys of Thanem again, and have to waste time rolling my up sleeves. My neck still stung from where she burned me. I wanted to be prepared if that happened again.

Or something worse.

"You ready?" Xander asked. I looked up into his eyes, and then past him, where Ilan was slumped against the rest of the packs.

"What about him?"

"He'll have his moment."

I squinted at him.

"You mean he, too, has an endless well of SanctusCraft to tap into? You're going to give him his own brand of chaos and see what happens?"

"No." Xander said. "Not likely."

"What then?"

"He's a Paladyr. Tough, but not very smart. Trained to act, not to reason." The grimace snuck across Xander's thin and weather-worn features. "I've put him in a *seawind bindweave*. To get out of it would be like untying ropes around his hands and ankles and pressing a boulder off of his chest. All at the same time."

I laughed.

"A test of strength, then?"

Xander nodded as we walked the hill. Daisey thumped to the earth behind us on her side, her belly fat with wild strawberries and bleached grass. If there were any left we'd find them. But I doubted there were any to be had. She seemed a thorough sort, if a bit slow and plodding and sleepy.

Bailey came to join Daisey and tried to get her to play with a nip on her back legs, but Daisey was already half asleep. Nurmedov gave Bailey a piroshok from a pouch at his side and followed behind us at an easy pace, eyes probing the mist. Hands ready at his sides in case his bow was called for.

"Ilan shows incredible promise." Xander said after a few minutes. He'd been thinking about the young man. Sorting through a Kalazaris-sized host of possibilities.

"But not with SanctusCraft?"

"No."

"TempusCraft?"

"Yes. He's already learned the basics of it in The Infernium. Of pushing the body to do things it can't do normally. Things it needs rigid training to achieve. But still *within* natural confines. But he has gifts and endowments. They're quite special. TempusCraft is nearly impossible without them. But some people get one gift. Others get ten. His gifts could even take him *beyond* natural confines."

"Really?"

That was a scary thought. Levitation? Flight? Passing through solid objects? Breathing under water? What did that mean?

There was a twitch in Xander's thin lips and he avoided saying something in favor of saying something else.

"Balance. Reflex. Size. Discipline." Xander nodded once after each word. "He has it all. And other things...he could even be one of the Shukach."

I went a bit numb to hear the word. It was imbued with lore. An ancient word. Older than Kalazaris or the path to it. I could imagine elaborate ceremonies. Legendary feats. An outfit that made his silver Paladyr armor and emerald green cape pale in comparison. A really cool helmet with a mask or something. Fierce and intimidating. Holy. Things Ilan had silently dreamed about as a kid surrounded by bald old men and their books.

The hill crested and we had to dig down to match the steep incline. I bent down once or twice to help the going with my hand. I think I heard Nurmedov whistling happily, but it could've just been the wind.

"Are you going to teach me?" I asked.

"Teach you what?"

"How to use this...touch? SanctusCraft."

Xander shook his head.

"That is the one thing I cannot teach you." The grimace returned. "You *know* that."

I sighed. So the path would be my teacher. The moment. The scent on the wind. The angle of the sun. All the things that were still mysteries to me. The imperfect process of the unknown hands of time.

"So it's not like the others?" I tried. "Other Crafts?"

Xander squinted down at me, silent for a moment.

"What *do* you know of Craft?"

"Not much. It was taboo at Bayh."

"But they were teaching MystisCraft there."

"They were?"

Xander nodded, rubbing his hands together.

"You didn't know?"

"No."

He laughed a quiet thing.

"Shows the power of MystisCraft, doesn't it? It can rule your life without you knowing it."

I stared at my feet for a moment.

"Can you explain?"

"Sure. The Mystis rules the Tempus. The Sanctus rules the Mystis, though most people never learn to touch it. To connect to it. But both the Mystis and Sanctus are locked *inside* of the Tempus. All three need each other to work properly. That's CovenCraft. Once, long ago, in a different time, it was *Covenant Craft*, but...again, that was a long time ago."

I gnawed on this for a moment. Especially considering that he was adept enough to leave his body but couldn't come back. And I had been adept enough to bring him back.

And that was before the deep well of my Sanctus had been opened up.

Xander continued.

"Bayh and places like it? They teach the power of the Mystis in order to avoid the Sanctus. In order to avoid all the things that could go wrong through that connection. The Mystis is much like Bayh, or even Kalazaris. A structure of walls and rooms and doors. Random particles milling about in some form of order and control. But the Sanctus? That's the sun and the stars in comparison. Wild *passionate* boundless energy. Nothing you can control. Only something you can hope to hold onto for a moment. Or a series of moments. A river, if you will, that goes to the sea. But if you go in that river you can't go in a boat. You're on your own. There's no vessel to transport you. It's just you and the river, and all rivers run to the sea. If you don't know how to swim, you drown. Simple as that. I know it's a scary thought, but to try to contain it in those terms limits it like our own eyes limit what we can see of the world. Because the horizon curves we cannot see past the vanishing point. We can only see so much. We can only go so far. There really is no end. No limit. No way to try to bind it within the walls of your Mystis."

Xander coughed twice, roughly, and reminded me that I hadn't heard him cough since waking him up back on the road to Kalazaris. I didn't like the nature of the cough. It had been stalking him and caught up with him.

He coughed again before speaking.

"Places like Kalazaris were built from the power of the Mystis, Rosalyn. But the earth itself is built from the power of the Sanctus."

I shivered at that. Scared at how deep the well within me was if it had the power to build a planet.

Was there an end to it?

No, he'd said as much. The only limit was the one my Mystis clamped upon it.

Strangely, I had already experienced that. I wondered at that as Xander continued, walking quickly so that I could barely keep up.

"Star paths are analyzed. Plants studied. Animals. The weather. It's the way of the Mystis. All those things you learned? All of those things you know? It's not all in vain. There is a purpose. But it just can't be the end of you. It can't be all there is to you. Or anyone. It's a citadel of walls and structures, like a large library of books. But your Sanctus?" He smiled. "That's a vast and endless sea. Like the one we just crossed. Who can know its depths? Who can know its end? Who can measure its volume, or dare to record the stories it has seen?" His tone darkened. "That's the blessing and the curse of it all. It's something to treat with...extreme caution."

I chewed on my lip. The hill flattened out but the sun-kissed pink mist did not. I was beginning to think the whole island, as long and spindly as it was, was covered in the obscuring mist. We could walk in circles and would never know. Or just come upon a mountain or a citadel.

Poof.

Or the mouth of the abyss. Just sitting there in the grass. With a sign that said *keep out.*

In that moment I had the knowing the island was enchanted, like, the *whole thing*, but didn't want to think about it. Xander had given me enough to think about.

And so I chanced one more question.

"SanctusCraft is more powerful than Tempus or MystisCraft, right? But...CovenCraft is more powerful than SanctusCraft?"

He nodded and said,

"More powerful than all three put together."

I finished the thought for him, hopefully to prove I wasn't a dull pupil.

"Because it *is* all three put together."

He nodded and I thought about it.

Covenant Craft...that was the covenant. The harmony, the balance, the inability to have one without the other. I remembered my geometric studies, and knew that it was MystisCraft to do so. To reach inside an image of the past to remember what I had learned and project it in front of me as if the study was real and alive.

CovenCraft instantly made sense.

It was a three-sided shape of three sides instantly joining together and thus becoming three-dimensional...and gaining a fourth face. A perfect an unbroken connection.

Of three triangles becoming a pyramid. Of a sphere sitting inside of that pyramid. Of that pyramid sitting inside of a cube. Of that cube sitting inside an octahedron.

All connected. Perfectly. Seamlessly.

And all the stars in the sky, and all the colors of the sun, and all the forces of nature...of water and fire and earth, flying around these cosmic connections in a balancing act of origin and destination, order and chaos.

And me, in the middle of that sphere, in the middle of it all, with the power to change it all if I wanted to.

Again, I shivered, and not for the air, which had grown much colder around us both.

TWENTY-THREE

She sat by a small fire, roasting fish. I couldn't smell it because, well, my sense of smell was never very good to begin with, but also because the salt wind of the sea was blowing away from us. The smoke of her cooking was woven into the pink mist, and she sat on the cold ground, cross-legged, in a small alcove of the hill as she cooked.

"Remember when I told you not to appear ignorant in front of Nurmedov?" Xander asked. I nodded. "This is quite the opposite. This is the time to be yourself, no matter what. If you're not, we'll never get where we need to."

I noticed Xander's ease as we approached the woman. I couldn't see much about her, through the mist. Though it was thinning, from a cloud to a veil, all I could see was a sheltered figure in an alcove on the hill so nice and cozy, roasting fish over a pit of angry orange coals.

"Why?"

"Because she's Feya."

I cocked my head to the side.

"Huh?"

"You know," Nurmedov said as he paced along side of us. I turned with a jump because I hadn't heard him sneak up. "Feya."

"No, I don't."

Nurmedov chuckled, his cheeks ruddier than ever and his beard looking trim and handsome. Strange how I could always look him in the eye. It made me like him more.

"Imagine that, X. She knows so much about so many things and nothing of the Feya?"

"It would appear that way, Nurmedov."

Nurmedov looked back to me.

"Wings. Wands. Wards. Knowledge of the unseen realm. Perfectly smoked cheese and a taste for pickles. Ships that sail in the clouds and drum chants that can unlock the gates of the land beneath the sea." He winked me a smile. "You know, Feya."

"Ohhh…" I drawled, staring at my feet for a moment. "Fairies."

It seemed a weak term for such a mighty race of creatures.

It made me wonder about humans and their relation to dwarves, elves, giants and the like. Fairies.

We could attain mighty feats if everything lined up properly and the right choices were made, for good or evil. But was it the same for a giant? Or a dwarf? Did every living creature abide by the same set of rules? Did they all have the same choices to make? The same will?

Because the Feya, well, they could do things I could only dream about, right?

Or things Xander hoped that I would learn to not say no to.

Again I wondered what he'd said about Ilan and his ability to maybe be one of the Shukach. Whoever they were. *Whatever* they were. I thought of a flying man with a steel face who could melt rocks with his eyes. I don't know why I thought that, but I did, and it made me feel small to think about the unknown and the unlocked potential of us all.

It humbled me.

Especially because I wanted to help. That's all I ever wanted to do. I want to heal the hurting. To mend the wounds. Fix the broken.

And to realize there was no end to that? That finally, for once, ability could actually *meet* and *exceed* desire?

I smiled.

"Greetings! " The woman said lyrically as we drew near. Nurmedov smiled and waved, and Xander grimaced, looking princely and stony in his ermine and black leather. I smiled, because, like my first moments with Daisey, I instantly liked her and wasn't going to fight that reaction.

She was a short and thin woman with sun-bronzed skin. Her almond-shaped eyes were dark brown like conditioned leather and her fat lips carried a sour expression. Her hair was long and dark brown, like her eyes, and bound in thick snake-like dreads that fell across her chest and back freely. She wore black from head to toe. A sleeveless tunic and a long cape that bunched at her feet, and soft boots to her knees. Her arms were inked with designs that I didn't understand. Flowers and faces and symbols. Her nose was pierced with a silver ring, as were her eyebrows with silver studs, and her ears were stretched with a hollow cork of carved ebony.

She was endlessly fascinating to me, like a field of wildflowers and honeybees in the forest.

"Them I know." She said, in a cute accent. She cast me a long glance. "But who might you be?"

"Rosalyn De Boswel." I said, opting not to extend my hand in a formal greeting. I didn't want to touch a Feya so quickly and find myself in an alternate dimension or watch her crumple on the ground or something. I had to be careful with my touch now.

The Feya smiled.

"In your tongue I am called Shmaila." She said. "I am happy to see you, Rosalyn. Are you hungry?"

"Always!" Nurmedov said, sitting down next to where she was. The heavy packs fell off his shoulders and he lounged, easy and broad, on the cold grass. Shmaila flashed Nurmedov a smile he didn't see. The adventurer leaned deep into the fire and inhaled the smoky scent, wafting it over his nose as he leaned back. The coals lit his face orange.

Nurmedov then stared deep into the fire, as diviners and mystics would to foretell the future.

"It's good to be home." He said to himself.

"You are from here?" I asked, sitting down across from Shmaila. Xander sat next to her, rather close.

"A traveler's home *is* the cooking fire." Shmaila said, slyly.

"I have some piroshki, if you'd like." Nurmedov offered her his pouch. "They're relatively fresh."

"I would like." Shmaila said sweetly and stoked the fire with a stick that wasn't really a stick. It was a forearm-length wand of birch. I marveled at how it slipped out of a fold in her cape with the flick of a wrist.

Nurmedov smiled into the fire as she rustled the coals just by pointing the wand. The wood never touched the coals. Not that it would've burned if it had. They seemed to arrange themselves like children in line for school. Shmaila set the pouch close to the fire to warm the piroshki.

"So, Xander...I have not seen you for a lifetime." She raised him a suspicious eyebrow. "What brings you to the gateway?"

"I have a favor to ask of you."

"Of *me*?"

"You are the guardian of the gate, are you not?"

Shmaila rolled her eyes and cast me a dark gaze across the fire.

"And here I thought he was going to apologize for last time." She turned back to Xander. "Ever so practical. And driven." A graceful hand brushed his ermine-clad shoulder, and then rested again, lovingly, but briefly, on his shoulder.

Then her hands were together in her lap as she hunched close to the fire to squint at the fish.

"When?" She said.

"As soon as you can."

"You can spend the night?"

"I'd rather not."

Shmaila's lips were sulky but her brown eyes were warm.

"But Rosalyn, she has so much to see. You would...rob her of these things?" She didn't even give Xander a chance at rebuttal and cast her wand in my direction. "You are a lover of knowledge, yes?"

I opened my mouth to say...

"You want to see things you have heard about in the whispers of others...things adventure-starved young men dream about when they go to bed for the night?"

I...

"You want see things that only happen once in a lifetime? Or in many lifetimes?"

I'm...

"You want to know of the Woven Worlds?"

I shot up and leapt back.

"Is she a Pryystys of Thanem?" I must've shouted. Nurmedov's cheeks were bulging with piroshok mid bite.

Shmaila laughed. It was a breathless spasm that leaned her into stony Xander for support.

My mouth twitched as a frown spread across my face.

"What?" I said. "What's so funny?"

"Oh, little girl, sit down." Shmaila patted the ground right beside her. "Come. Come on." She beckoned with her hand, opening and closing like a door.

I sniffed my misunderstanding in my sleeve and excused myself past Nurmedov, who used me as a shield to steal a fillet of smoked fish. Shmaila glared at him for a moment and put her arm around me as I sat down next to her. She was the opposite of Xander. Warm and bubbly, small and affectionate.

"Rosalyn." She said, in her musical accent. "Feya do not concern themselves with things of this earth like Pryystyses or Paladyrs. Like Kings and Queens and Princes and Princesses. Like Nurmedov, we are travellers. Adventurers. But ours is not merely of this earth. But of all earths. Of all worlds. Of all realms. Of the unseen and the unknown. The untouched. We are...friends, if you will, to those who wish to travel the sacred paths for that purpose which is allowed by them."

She smiled at the expression Xander grimaced at. At my features, frozen in thought. Shmaila squeezed my shoulder and began to rub it aimlessly as she talked, casting a hand to the sky. The pinkish mist dissipated. Only the cooking fire was left.

We could see far beyond into the valley. A windswept sea of bleached grass. The sky above was icy blue, the color of Nurmedov's eyes.

"The Woven Worlds allow themselves to be manipulated by those who inhabit them. For love and virtue...for hate and evil. They are, like the night sky, a living canvas of constant energy. Uncontrollable comsic energy. Malleable, yes, but not controllable."

"This is very good trout." Nurmedov interrupted, picking a bone from his teeth.

"Consider yourself, Rosalyn. If the earth moaned and groaned and the mountains shook, and the earth split wide open as your skin would if cut by a sword, would you not want to heal it? To seal it up and mend it and make it brand new?"

"I would." I said.

"And you can. The Woven Worlds would respond to your touch." Her fingertip kissed my nose, before returning to the blue sky to draw a shape. To Craft. "And if you carried a heart of hatred, would you not see that tear in the earth as you saw the tear in your own soul? Would you not flood that tear with your rage and hatred and anger?"

I squinted as a small, dark cloud formed in the sky where she had drawn it.

"I would." I said.

"And, again, the Woven Worlds would respond to your touch."

She pulled the cloud to us. It was a rain cloud, fat and full of water, and she set it right above Nurmedov's head as he munched on her roasted trout.

Water poured down upon him as if from a spilled bucket and he shot up out of his seat in the grass and ran off down the hill as the rain cloud followed him.

Shmaila again laughed her breathless spasm, leaning into Xander.

Then Shmaila sighed, letting her eyes fall into the fire.

"We seek the mysteries of the future. We have no idea what it holds for us all. But we also protect the future from those we deem to be unworthy to shape it."

"How?" I asked.

"The day is young. Not so many questions so early." She said, shaking her head so that her long dreads flopped back and forth. "Please, eat some fish. I hear it is very good."

Xander reached into the fire and picked up a coal. My heart leapt in my throat to watch it, but it was just a trained reaction. His hand cupped the raging coal, and steam poured out from his knuckles. Then he opened his hand and the coal was a stone. Black. Like the eyes in his skull. Stone cold and dead.

"Do you deem me worthy to shape the future, yet again, Shmaila?"

The Feya woman looked away, hurt. Her nostrils flared and she stood up, quickly, and let her eyes dig out into the mist that sat on the edge of the horizon. Across the uneven expanse of bleached sea grass. As far as the eye could see.

She blinked a few times, still distant, and then sighed and sat back down. Her body was hunched, her gaze glowering into the flames.

"If only you could be guaranteed to find what you're looking for down there."

My eyes snapped between Xander and Shmaila. Xander's face was glazed with pain. Old pain. Secret pain. The very thing that crippled him so bad to talk about. The reason he'd left his Tempus and found he couldn't come back. Until I had brought him back.

"I've looked everywhere." He nearly whispered. Then he shrugged in defeat. "Everywhere I could think of."

Shmaila placed her hand on his shoulder once again and squeezed, her sullen lips twisted in sorrow.

"I will open the gates of the abyss for you once and never will I open them again."

Shmaila turned to me with a smile. Hollow though it was, it made me feel like the embers of the cooking fire were deep in my belly.

"He will go...but will you stay here with me?" She asked.

I blinked in shock. For some reason I thought I *had* to go with Xander.

But why? I'd never thought about it.

Still the rigid teaching of the Nomyd Creed? That *one who saved a life was compelled to keep it*?

Or was it my own thirst for knowledge and exploration, hungry to see the ends of the earth and know its mysteries?

Or was it a bit of everything? A bit of the unexplainable? That something that would define me sat just in front of me, dark and heavy, and I just had to walk into that moment and touch it and it would all make sense.

I looked at Xander for a moment. Xander who said nothing. Who stared in the fire. Who looked tired but still very stately and noble in his narrow and needle-like sort of way.

He'd provoked me to smash the vessel bottling up my Sanctus without me knowing, but he'd *asked* me to join him in the abyss because I could bring him back.

Back to what?

My eyes darted to the fire before meeting the Feya's gaze again. It burned in me like the coals at our feet. I figure if I looked into Shmaila's eyes for too long I would melt like butter on kasha. I would melt into her hands and she could work me and weld me and shape me into something far greater than I was.

Into something I only dreamed of being.

"Where are the gates to the abyss?" I asked, quietly.

"On the other side of the island." She said. "It will take a few hours to get there."

I nodded and swallowed the dryness in my throat.

"Then that is when I will decide."

TWENTY-FOUR

We hadn't walked that far when the pink mist began to burn orange, and the hills rolled and dipped and swayed. Wind kissed the near-white grass, and rustled its long stalks. Now and then, I dropped my hands down to my sides and let the bleached wheat tickle my fingertips, wondering if I could touch anything and change it. A river? A lake? A mountain? Could I reach up into the sky and touch a star? Was this ability limited to flesh and bone?

Or could something touch *me* too? Did reaching out and absorbing the energy of this seemingly empty and enchanted land impart something to me? Could I take it and harness it? Is that what Xander did with the weather to make a sword of ice, or what the Pryystys did to Nurmedov's arrow to make a shield of ash? Was it simply a matter of manipulating what already was for your own purpose?

I wondered at the motive. *That* was the danger. Shmaila said as much. The Woven Worlds responded to those who shaped them.

For love and virtue.

For hatred and evil.

It was a lot to think about. After what I'd seen and done. The choice to stay or go still churning within.

All mixed up and twisted. Tumbling around and wrestling thoughts and feelings.

Till we reached a wide plain, perfectly flat and even as far as the eye could see. No mist. Just the unfiltered orange sun, reaching high in the sky and just about to burn afternoon yellow.

At the base of the plain was the largest mountain I'd ever seen, nearly a perfect triangle. An earthen temple of blue black obsidian.

But my eyes only skipped over the giant mountain and its blue diamond peak.

Because Ilan was in the middle of the plain.

He was standing like a statue, waiting. I didn't know how long he'd been there. Xander said he had extraordinary TempusCraft. Maybe he just sneezed and he was there. It made sense to me. There was so much I didn't understand. Maybe hurricanes were just people sneezing in other parts of the world. Hex if I know.

"Oh good." Nurmedov smiled. "Was wondering when the beauty rest was up." Then Nurmedov added cheekily to Shmaila, "He's a lot bigger when you stand next to him."

Shmaila only squinted at the adventurer in a way that shut him up.

I wanted to believe there was some mystique to Ilan, but I knew him. I *knew* him. As much as I was fighting the memory that I didn't. I had to hold onto it. *Had* to.

He was a big man with little dreams. His eyes had grown colder. His voice rougher. But he was *still* Ilan, whatever that really meant, deep down, he was still Ilan and I was still Rosy.

Ilan and Rosy.

Wind and Rain. Sun and Stars.

We all waited on the crest of the hill. It was a moment frozen in time. He stood there patiently for whatever challenge was about to come his way. Emotionlessly.

That was the Paladyr in him.

"I'll handle this." I said, and stepped forward. Xander's grip was tight on my arm.

"No." He said. "His time has come."

"What?" I said, wrenching my arm away. When he didn't answer, I said, "Why do you have to be so cryptic?"

Xander still ignored me and looked to Shmaila.

"I think he may be one of the Shukach."

The Feya raised one eyebrow and crossed her arms.

"Strong words, Xander. The Shukach have not taken on a new pupil in hundreds of years."

Xander's expression darkened with a passing grimace.

"New pupils are good for the soul."

"But the Shukach are strict."

"He's special."

"Correction. *Very* strict."

"Trust me when I say they would bend over backwards to teach this boy their ways."

"Boy?"

"Seventeen, I think."

"Seventeen and with such promise? Do tell."

"Well..." Xander scratched his chin. "The boy is afraid of flight...but, he broke out of the hold I placed him in on the beach."

"Out of one of your holds?" Shmaila smiled. "With TempusCraft alone?" Her laughter was a small bubble and her eyes were no longer warm and inviting but instantly predatory. Hungry. "Oh, apt indeed. This should be fun."

Nurmedov sighed heavily.

"You guys are all nuts. Just let *me* talk to him."

We all looked at Nurmedov and his cheeks reddened.

"What?" He said. "I felt that we had an understanding."

Still no one bought what Nurmedov was selling.

"You know, a guy thing."

"You mean a peacock thing." Xander said.

"More like a rooster thing." Shmaila corrected, and tapped the adventurer on the shoulder. "It's okay. It won't take long."

"You could go wrangle the dragons." Xander said.

"Heh..." Nurmedov turned around and walked away, snipping off a piece of grass with one of his knives and sticking it between his teeth. I marveled at the quickness.

The fluid motion. Arm down then up, knife out, knife back and sheathed as the grass found its place between his teeth. I frowned and wondered. Did Nurmedov have any sort of Craft?

Or was he just...normal?

Ha! If Nurmedov was normal then we were all relatively insane.

Shmaila had yet to take a step and I bit my lip before asking again.

"Please, can't I talk to him?"

"About what?"

"About...all this?"

"What is this?"

"I mean..." I sighed. "About me. About who I am. What I've become."

Shmaila turned her melting gaze to me.

"Didn't he witness your Craft with the Pryystys? Didn't you already try to talk to him and he attacked you?"

I felt my mouth slip open and dissolve into my chin.

"How on earth did you know that?"

Her musical voice turned to stone and she spoke very slowly, failing to blink.

I was hypnotized.

"The Feya are a species of extreme dissociative paradox, abiding outside of time, inhabiting parallel dimensions and alternate realities..."

Then Shmaila laughed her breathless cascade, falling into Xander's shoulder. Even Xander smiled.

"I'm kidding, child, I'm kidding. Xander told me. Relax. Don't be so serious."

I frowned at the laughter but she was right. *Don't be so serious.*

Relax.

I squinted up at the sun. That giant ball of fire. For some reason, that's what I wanted to tell Ilan. Lighten up. Don't be so serious. Remember that thing up there? The sun? Yeah, that thing we used to run around beneath after studies, chasing butterflies and crickets and frogs? That thing that would burn our skin year after year if we saw too much of it but we'd never learn. There was too much life to live, out there, together. Just you and me, just beyond the walls of Bayh where the courtyard opened up to the creek...where the light stuck its fingers through the birches no matter what the season.

I dropped my head to hide my quivering lip and the single tear I shed.

Yeah, I didn't want to say all that. Not with his hard Paladyr face set for war. I knew he wouldn't get it. Couldn't get it.

We were far too much alike, he and I, and like me, he would have to learn his lesson the hard way.

Mine was the shattering of whatever bind in my Mystis disrupted my powerful connection to SanctusCraft.

So whatever then was his?

TWENTY-FIVE

Shmaila set her eyes upon the sun and waved her hands. It was an intricate dance, one hand at a time. They would cross and her fingers would flutter, then her arms would rise up in a perfect mirror of each other. Her hands would twist and constrict.

She was transforming herself.

I stifled a small gasp as her clothes dissolved away and her body became something like liquid light. As if sunlight had been poured into the shape of her body. Wings spread from back her like strips of honey. She had six wings.

Xander all but lifted an eyebrow and the salty wind raked across us.

Then Shmaila let the long black cape go.

I watched as it twisted and curled like a fallen leaf. Rising. Rising. Rising.

Shamila produce her wand and flicked it towards the cape. It became a flock of bats. Screeching and batting their wings in chaos.

Ilan saw this and drew his sword. Warm sunlight kissed the runes and made them glow. The ash shield slipped from his back, and he hefted it against Shmaila as I had against him. In some vain hope it would help him. He had lost his helmet, but still had the rest of his silver armor. It looked dull. Tarnished.

And his emerald green cape was but a waxy leaf shuddering against the winds of a rising tempest.

Xander raised his hand and the wind shifted, blasting against him for a moment, before turning the other way. Pushing the bats. Driving them through the cloudless sky.

Sunfire-glazed Shmaila walked forward, one step at a time. Ilan stared her down, crouching and waiting. Keeping his focus.

"Whatever you do, do *not* interfere." Xander said to me. He was still controlling the wind. He would control it throughout the battle.

Interference? I wouldn't dream of it. And even if I wanted to, what could I possibly do? They were both too far away to touch.

"She will not hurt him." I peeped. "Will she?"

"Rosalyn..." Xander's features were sad and worn. "It is far easier to take a blow to the cheek than a blow to one's pride. Broken bones can heal, but a broken mirror must be replaced. He will have to see what he really is, and not what he wants to be."

Xander trailed off at the end. I didn't know if he had more to say or couldn't. Again I felt whatever wound he was harboring rise within him. It was truly crippling and he sat down on the grass.

I stood. They were but a hundred paces from each other. Soon there would be no turning back.

"You're scaring me."

"Why?"

"Because you're not the one fighting him." I said. "You're all soft inside. You're just a big soft powdered sweet roll who forgot how to smile. But her? She's a Feya. She could kill us all with a single thought. It's not fair."

"Life is not fair, Rosalyn."

I crossed my arms.

"And you, whatever your problem is, whatever wounds you're carrying around like a stillborn child, do you want that for him?"

Xander inhaled the cold air he controlled as if it stung. He looked away, hugging his knees to his chest.

"Some save their own skin. Others shed their skin to save others."

More cryptic nonsense. I rubbed my forehead.

"You don't see, you're making his decision for him, *just* like you did with me. *That's* what's not fair. You're pushing him down in a hole so that he'll fight back. You're provoking him to be something *you* want him to be. You're…"

"Shut up, Rosalyn." Xander growled. "Your Mystis is showing."

My throat made something of an angry hot teakettle noise and I took a pace from him and stared down into the plain.

Whatever. They were puppet masters. Shaping the Woven Worlds as they saw fit. They wanted Ilan to be one of these Shukach folks and were probably going to push him to death's door to test how strong he was naturally. To see if he had what it took. And that was just their test, right? Heaven knew what the Shukach folks, whoever the Hex they were, would do to him once they indoctrinated him in their mystical ways.

And I resented them for it.

I resented them all.

Maybe someday I'd see their wisdom, but not now. *Not* now.

"You have drawn steel on my island." Shamila said, her voice the thunder of a waterfall. "What is the meaning of this?"

Ilan held a defensive posture, one foot in front of the other, round shield protecting the middle of his body, sword low. Blue eyes snapped up to see the seemingly random flight of the bats, the distraction they were, and back to the advancing figure of flame and sun that Shmaila had become.

"I have come to free Rosalyn De Boswel from her spell!" He shouted back.

I was crushed. Xander looked up at me as more tears fell from my eyes. No hiding it now.

If I analyzed the split second he threw his weapon at me, I could've seen it was the flat of his blade. To knock me out. To haul me back to The Infernium. To cure me.

Yes, it was a big thing for him. To break the rules to try and save me. CovenCrafters were to be killed. Not mended and healed. Not restored. So maybe there was a bit of Nomyd left in him after all. Nomyd *and* friend. But it was so tainted. Tainted to think The Infernium held the answer to anything other than cold-blooded murder.

"I have come to take her back!" He shouted. "And I will not leave without her!"

"Back to where?" Shmaila growled, raising her arms.

The grass shuddered as all the bats descended in the shape of a giant sickle.

It was breathtaking.

Ilan's blue eyes were swollen in his sockets, and he reacted to the sickle of bats. But not before he said,

"Bayh."

Ilan dove and tucked and rolled. Wheat grass exploded in dry shards to receive the sickle of bats where he had been standing. They cut a ribbon through the earth, digging out a scar of rich black dirt.

And by the time Ilan came to his feet again, the woman was upon him. No longer made of the sun but back again as she had been just a few moments ago. A small and fierce Feya clothed in black, her bare arms inked with art and symbols, her dark eyes warm and alive.

Ilan's heart must've exploded in his chest to see the bats fly back to Shmaila and form themselves into her black cape once again.

I know mine did.

I sat down beside Xander with wet eyes.

"Why?" I whined to myself. "Why...?"

Back to Bayh...back to *Bayh*? Not to Kalazaris? So that meant...that he wanted to run away from The Infernium? And seeing me was the thing that made him want to do it? That *I* had provoked what he must've been thinking about doing the moment he signed his life away?

I was the catalyst of his regret.

And it didn't matter now.

He belonged to Xander and Shmaila and whatever test they had in mind.

He belonged to the battle that was about to break him.

TWENTY-SIX

Shmaila flicked her wand at him and it stretched in her hand to become a staff. She twisted it around her head three times and smashed it into the ground.

Ilan hopped back as tongues of flame licked through the grass. The salt wind drove them. Rolling toward him like rising tide. Ilan braced himself behind the shield of ash as the ripple of fire splashed across him. He tucked and rolled, slicing a swathe of burning grass around him, standing tall in a charred circle.

Shmaila whirled the staff again and smashed it into the ground, and it ruptured the ground, tossing Ilan into the air. I was in awe at the ease in which his large body arced lazily through the fury of smoke and charred grass, and the grace in which he tumbled and bounced up, right in front of Shmaila.

And then the fight was on.

Ilan's swordplay was swift and refined, and I bit my hand to think what it'd be like if he trained for another year or two or ten. I never thought the boy I'd spent my life with was one born to wield a sword.

Ilan drove her back and it shocked me. His body bloomed in combat. Opening up as did a bird of prey in flight, or a tiger on the hunt. To watch him was...I couldn't describe it. It was nearly beautiful. It was the definition of TempusCraft.

His movements were a blur, marked by the clang and clatter of sword, shield, and staff. Shmaila's eyes were wide to stave off his combat.

It was relentless.

And there was art in it. He knew when to press, and when to recede, as did a musician lost in their instrument. He splashed like rainwater, sliced like winter wind, and jabbed with the power and ease of sunlight through a forest. He twisted his body in ways that would've made me fall helplessly on my back, only to spring up and launch another series of attacks. Jumping and kicking, throwing his sword and shield at Shmaila. His war was linked, each move a series of chains in one endless tapestry of violence.

Shmaila countered his every move as if she knew what he'd do before he even did, but Ilan fought on bravely, refusing to give in.

Because he wanted me back?

Or because his life depended on it?

Xander manipulated the smoke from the harmless fires behind him to sting his eyes. Sometimes the thick black smoke would wrap around him like a pair of hands. He would duck and roll and throw his blade where Shmaila had been, only to correct his error just a moment before Shmaila's staff would've smacked him upside the head.

Around and around they danced and spun, drawing closer and closer to us, as Ilan pushed Shmaila back under the watchful gaze of the sun.

His emerald green cape unfurled behind him as he feinted a jab to Shmaila's gut and threw his sword and shield above his head to cross block the overhand crash of her staff.

Ilan grit his teeth not to crumple under the blow. I gasped as shockwaves rippled through the grass.

In a flash, Shmaila wheeled the staff around to club him in the side but instead of receding as he had done when Shmaila dealt him one of those thunderous blows, Ilan leapt forward. He barely cleared the swoop of her staff, landing next to her exposed flank.

Ilan lashed out with his sword and a backbreaking contortion saved Shmaila from being cloven in half.

But as she stood up again to attack, the ash shield smashed her in the face.

Xander stood up, fists clenched. I stared at him. Was he smiling? Was it disbelief?

Ilan whipped his sword behind him in a reverse grip and pressed his hands together, as if making one weapon. A sword hidden by a shield. He crouched and rolled and spread his body wide as Shmaila flailed with her staff, catching the air where Ilan had been.

But Ilan was behind her. With the momentum of his arms flung wide, he did what I hoped he wouldn't.

He leapt in the air, arching his back, falling like a bolt of lighting as Shmaila turned, features cloaked with fear.

The ash shield stunned her, smacking her face. But it was the sword that got her. Reaching around in a roundhouse, hidden in that strange reverse grip, Shmaila didn't see it till it was upon her.

And it would've taken her head right off.

But Ilan slashed the air where Shmaila had been. Where she was no longer.

Because Xander was no longer next to me.

I hadn't even felt him go. He just went. He was here, then he was there, with Shmaila in his arms, standing a pace from Ilan.

Ilan twisted the sword around to his standard grip and Xander held out a hand. Shmaila's nose was bleeding and her forehead was glazed with sweat. I didn't understand. Wasn't she a Feya?

What...

I found myself running. Ilan was running. Not at Shmaila. At Xander. Xander was protecting Shmaila with his body. Shielding her.

Ilan reached out with fiery yellow silver. The blade was alive in his hand. Hungry. Xander had no weapon. Just his hands. The blade rose. Xander threw out his arm. The blade fell.

The blade connected on his bracer with a scatter of sparks.

I couldn't run fast enough. Shmaila was behind him, wiping her nose. Sniffing. Staring at her own blood on an open palm.

Ilan would not stop. The blade spun through the air and caught Xander again on the bracer with a shower of hot sparks.

My lungs burned. I threw myself across the sway of the grass.

I was almost upon them.

Ilan threw his blade at Xander who stepped aside and cuffed him on the ear. Ilan yelped and spun around as his ear began to trickle dark red.

No! No! No! My eyes teared as I ran. *Why does everyone have to fight! Why? It doesn't make sense! Stop it! STOP IT!*

Ilan roared and threw himself at Xander. Xander smacked him in the nose and dodged the blade to slap him across the face.

I reached Xander first. Xander, the stone statue of black leather and white ermine. I used his shoulder to propel past him, to break up the fight, just as Ilan turned.

Rage possessed his face. Pain and anger. In a blur he spun and undercut the blade straight for Xander's belly.

But I was in the way.

The blade tore right through me before I had a chance to speak. To say no. To say anything.

To say I'm sorry.

Sorry, for what? I don't know. For whatever I did that made him run away from me.

But I couldn't say a thing.

My lungs squelched. I coughed and staggered back. The horizon lurched. Suddenly it was as if that massive mountain of blue-black obsidian was near enough to touch.

Ready to slide right over the top of me. To keep me entombed in freezing cold pain.

I felt all of their eyes on me. The fight had ceased.

Xander's face was pale, nearly as white as his cloak. Shmaila stepped forward and Xander stopped her as I pulled the sword from my body. It fell to the ground with a dull thud. Shmaila pressed forward again and Xander shook his head emphatically. Ilan was too shocked to do anything.

But not as shocked as he was when I put my hands to my stomach to stop the bleeding.

Ilan threw his hands before his face as the light of a dying star exploded across my skin.

Pain ebbed. Receding like the tide. I sighed as if I had been jerked straight from a nightmare and realized I was going to be okay.

I pulled my hands away and the skin beneath my torn tunic was peach colored and perfect.

Shmaila stood up straight and seemed to glow, smiling at Xander.

He only nodded.

But Ilan. He staggered forward as if *he* was the one who had a Paladyr rune sword shoved through his body. His face was free of the anger I'd seen only moments ago. His blue eyes were reddened with sorrow, and he fell upon me in a loose embrace, his sobs coming slow and heavy.

And though I hated it, I knew.

Ilan Braun had been broken. His rare gifts of TempusCraft had been forged in one thing, and tempered in another.

And if he never forgot who was worthy of the edge of his sword, he would be one of the few to shape the Woven Worlds indeed.

I hugged Ilan and he hugged me back fiercely. My cheeks were wet with his tears and his with mine. It had been a long time. Too long. But not long enough to forget just how much we needed each other.

And how, where we were headed, we'd need each other more than we ever had.

TWENTY-SEVEN

When Nurmedov arrived, all three furry dragons marching happily behind him, he stopped and squinted across the scorched plain.

"Shoulda let me talk to him." He said.

Daisey tipped her snout to the wind and a puff of sea breeze raked across her long gray beard and made her look wise. Behind her, Bailey rolled in the grass to itch his back and stood up to nip at the wheat spores his thrashing had caused to rise like bleached snow. Nilius did nothing, some large cottony shrub with black eyes that probed the distance.

Shmaila left to go see the dragons. Xander was deep in conversation with Ilan, who kept wiping his tear-slick cheeks. Both were out of earshot. The rune sword was still on the ground, where it had fallen after I'd pulled it from my own belly.

My blood was still on it.

Nurmedov wandered over, hand on one of his daggers. The amber one.

"So...what happened?"

"Too much to summarize."

"I'm patient."

I said nothing and tried to replay it all in my Mystis but it was a blur. Just a smear of frantic motion and color. A supernova. A beautiful stain. An explosion of light.

I scratched my forehead.

"Umm...can I ask you a question?"

He cocked his head and let a wry smile spread across his lips.

"Sure thing."

I sighed. Might as well just let it out.

"What do *you* want me to do?"

"What do you mean?"

I didn't want to explain it to him because that required thinking, and he seemed like the only guy who wasn't on some sort of Craft, which meant he was the only guy with a clear head and a clean conscience.

"Xander wants me to go to the abyss. Ilan wants me to go to Bayh. Shmaila wants me to stay here. But you?" I looked him square in the eye. "What do *you* want me to do?"

"I want you to tell me what Shmaila did with the rest of the fish."

I punched his arm. He said *ow* and I rolled my eyes.

"Seriously."

"I am being serious. It's very good fish and I'm still hungry."

I laughed and he took a step closer to me and looked over his shoulder. Shmaila was tickling Bailey's ribs with her wand and Daisey had flopped down for a nap, her belly heaving with deep breaths, her legs sticking straight out in front of her as her wings were splayed straight out behind her. I could see her missing teeth. Ilan was nodding as Xander was talking. Xander had retrieved the rune sword and held it between them with his palms flat. My blood was no longer on it.

"I'll answer your question if you answer mine first."

I sighed and said I would.

"What do you gain by asking me?"

I searched his face and thought about it. His icy blue eyes and ruddy cheeks, his neatly trimmed beard and light brown hair. His pragmatism and purpose, ruined by his incurable sense of humor. The stories he could tell if he would only be serious for a moment. The peril he'd seen. The places he'd been.

"What do I *gain* by asking you?"

"Yeah."

"Honesty. Impartiality."

"Is it worth that much to you?"

"Yes." I nodded. "It is."

"And you think I can give it? When you have masters and apprentices of Craft left and right? You want to know what *I* think?"

"Yes, Nurmedov. I want to know what you think. I want you to be the sun that you worship for a moment. Expose all the shadows in this crazy mess without giving a damn about the consequences."

He bit his lip and nodded. His eyes scanned around the sea of grass behind me. The black pyramid of a mountain loomed large on the curve of the earth.

"I want you to go with us...to the abyss."

"Why?"

"Because, reasons."

"Don't pull a muscle trying to explain yourself."

"No, I'm serious."

"You're never serious."

"Truly, I am. The reason is...I don't know, just as big as any of the stuff you've heard out of anyone else's mouth in the past twenty-four hours."

"Really?"

"Yeah."

"Like...the shaping of worlds?"

He nodded slowly and met my gaze. Something told me he wasn't joking. That he wasn't the explaining type. A joke was always easier. Perhaps because he didn't know how to quantify it all.

"That big?"

"Yup. That's why I'm here. Do you think I'd leave Kalazaris for anything other than a world-defining moment? I mean, seriously Rosalyn, I have a pretty cushy place in the temple. Everyone likes me and the food is great. I never get dirty and everyone smells nice. Why would I leave all that unless something really *really* big compelled me to?"

My eyebrows were scrunched up and I looked at my hands. What would they be touching in the abyss? What awaited me...*us* that was so incredible?

"You've got a point." I peeped. "And...well, shouldn't I know more? More details?"

"Don't you know enough?"

"Xander only said because I can bring him back. Is that not the end of it?"

"Maybe not."

"What do you mean?"

"Do you ever wonder why he needs someone to bring him back?"

I didn't. I was still making sense of myself. And I didn't think that was going to stop soon. I would be forever awakening from blindness.

"I figured it was beyond me." I shrugged. "I'm only fifteen."

"Never use your age as an excuse to be ignorant." He corrected. Then he added, "I'm almost thirty and I still know next to nothing about life."

I smiled.

"You know what I'm saying."

"No, Rosalyn." He pulled out his dagger and held it between us. "You're sharper than the edge of this weapon, and you're going to need every bit of that if you choose to go down there. You can't blindly follow Xander just waiting to bring him back. If you go down there, not knowing what you're getting into, then *you* won't be coming back."

Nurmedov waited for me as I chewed on this. Sure, if I marched up to Xander and said, *hey, what the Hex? Tell me everything*...and he gave me some answer that would satisfy my need to know in the moment, I could very well be eating up a big fat lie. Nurmedov was telling me to be sensitive, to be cool, to be still and to listen.

To figure it out.

In essence, he was telling me *not* to trust Xander.

When I looked him in the eyes again he nodded very slowly.

"Now you're getting it." He tapped the hilt of the dagger on my heart. "You *know* what I mean. And when the time comes, you'll *know* what to do."

He sheathed his dagger.

"I'll go a step further before you ask me." He said, making sure Xander was rapt in his conversation with Ilan. "I'll tell you why *I'm* going."

I could barely hear his whisper as he turned to collect the dragons once again.

But what I heard scared the snot out of me.

"I have unfinished business." He said. "With someone named Ozmander."

TWENTY-EIGHT

Ilan fell in step next to me as we all walked to the perfect triangle-shaped mountain, rising straight up from the earth like the head of a blue-black spear. Forced up from the abyss.

And whatever went on down there.

Yes, it didn't take The Learnyd to see what was staring us all right in the eyes.

The pyramid mountain was the door to the abyss.

"You okay?" Ilan asked.

I tapped my belly where the sword had gone in. My rags of an outfit were getting pretty worn out by now. The slit where the sword had gone through was still in my clothes, but my skin and organs were perfectly healed.

"Never better."

He shook his head and said,

"Listen, I..."

"Ilan, it's okay." I cut him off. "I know how you feel. Kind of. I mean, I know I got it all wrong back in Kalazaris, but I never expected to see you again. And to see...how much you've changed."

The ghost of a smile crossed his river eyes and made his square-jawed face look a bit sly.

"I'm not the only one."

"Yeah, well, most of the time I feel like I'm just holding on for dear life."

"Most?"

"Yeah." I combed my hair behind my ears. "But sometimes it feels like symmetry and harmony. Like it all lines up and I've got the right answer. But those moments are just a spark."

"Really? What's the rest?"

"Walking in darkness."

His hand fell to his sword, idly playing with the hilt. The ash shield was still on his back. It seemed like so long ago the Pryystys had formed it out of Nurmedov's arrow. As we walked, I chewed on it. Could I do that? Yes. I could do *more* than that. Yet there was nothing specific to think about, nothing like a sword or shield to focus on. To work or weld. Just the knowledge that I held within me the quantifiable substance to wrought change. After all, hadn't I done that with my own body? Seal up and heal tissue with a flash of light?

But the thing that got me was the *moment itself*. Like *it* was in control. Not me. My Sanctus had leapt out and touched that river-to-the-sea connection Xander talked about. Without my knowledge or consent. It'd just...happened. In a flash. And maybe I could learn to work with that and then the sky could be the limit. Or...the stars. Or maybe there were no limits. I didn't know.

But what I did know, was there was a *moment* that defined that connection. That sparked it.

Just as I had said.

The rest was walking in darkness.

Ilan wiped his brow. His armor clinked as he walked.

"Thank heavens." He said, as we passed into the shadow of the mountain. The coolness was apparent. To me, it went from cold to colder, but Ilan had always been hot blooded. And, well, he did fight a Feya not too long ago. He wasn't breathing hard, but he'd worked up a sweat.

Oh yeah, and there had been fire, too.

Maybe they'd still be fighting if I hadn't intervened. Or whatever I had done.

Which reminded me...

"Ilan...I don't remember you being so..." He smiled as I searched for the word, knowing I was speaking of his skill with the sword. "Competent."

He laughed.

"Yes, well, when I ran away from Bayh, I learned a lot."

"Like what?"

His tone was humble.

"The road is a brutal master."

"The road taught you how to fight?"

"In one sense, yes. The road taught me grit. A gentleman may fight elegantly, but a warrior fights to survive." Ilan sighed to ponder a few memories. That grit he talked about was in his voice now, and it wouldn't leave. It was growing stubble and dark on his face. Shadowing his river eyes. Throwing a swagger to his gait. There was no denying his transformation.

From a cub to a wolf.

"But you *do* fight elegantly." I said, and he checked my smile to see the pride in it.

"I prefer *efficiently*, but thank you. I..." He scratched his eyebrow. I don't know why he was still trying to be delicate with me. All the cards were on the table now. "I..."

"Ilan, it's okay. In my mind, we're not Ilan and Rosy anymore. I mean..." I threw my hands up in the air. "We still are, but we aren't? You know?"

"Yeah."

"I'm not like, forget all that's gone on between us, but really, we're both in the hands of something far greater than we ever imagined. This momentum we're in is unstoppable. We're back together again, but we have to ride it out before we can talk about the way things were or the way things are going to be."

"What about me running away?"

"What about it?"

"Do you resent me becoming a Paladyr?"

I shrugged.

"That's what I'm trying to say, I guess. Instead of thinking of you as once having been a Paladyr, I see you as...about to become one of the Shukach."

"I don't know about that." He murmured. "They sound pretty extreme."

"More so than The Infernium?"

"Killers are killers." He nearly whispered. "Whether you slay giant pit vipers that steal children from their beds or bent-backed old CovenCrafters that sell herbs in the street market, killing *is* killing."

"Ilan, you *didn't* kill me."

"But I almost did. And I'll never forget it."

"I think that's the point." I bit my lip. "...Maybe we shouldn't talk about it."

"Do you want to talk about the abyss instead?" He said, sardonically.

"Yes. I gather you're going with us?"

"Only to see you safely back to Bayh."

I nodded and smiled. My assent comforted him. I touched his shoulder and squeezed.

"I'll protect you from whatever's down there, Rosy."

"Thank you."

"I promise you it *won't* be elegant."

I nodded again.

But as we walked and walked I thought more about it. I didn't know if I wanted to go back to Bayh.

I got the concept, though. He wanted to say he was done with his lashing out at the four walls that had raised him and confined him. But he had gotten sick on the big bad world and craved the peace and stillness of the birches near the creek, and the evening sun. The cool of the day. All that he remembered about Bayh.

Because in his rapid overexposure to the world, all he could remember about Bayh were the good things.

And all the memories had me in them.

Out on the road to Kalazaris and in the city itself, his eyes had seen horrible things. Far too many of them by his own hand.

But my eyes were opening wider and wider and wider to the immutable clarity of the Woven Worlds and I didn't want to go back to those four walls and go blind again.

We'd talk about it later.

TWENTY-NINE

Shmaila led us into the mountain through an opening I could see was formed by human hands, or at least human thought. Runes were carved on the giant trapezoidal opening, more of a warning to the unaware, I guessed. *Keep out if you don't belong.* It looked ancient and well perseveed, leeward to the salty sea wind. I couldn't read them, but Shmaila paid them no attention. We were all following her now.

The carved opening was big enough for the dragons to fit through easily and so were the long passageways that stretched out before us. Shmaila flicked her wand and torches lit themselves, illuminating the length of our path. The walls were made of colored tiles...mosaics. Just to gaze at them was to see the sordid history of something. What, I couldn't tell. There were strange mixed creatures, armored trees with spears, giants with weapons of bone and birds made of clouds. Mountains spewed fire and mages that controlled the waves to make swords and shields and fought each other as one defended a city, and another defended a fleet of ships that covered the sea like black mold.

I lost my breath a bit as the immensity of the shape slid over us and stretched around us.

We were going *inside* of the black pyramid mountain.

"This is nothing." Shmaila said as she walked beside me. "Just wait till I open the doors to the abyss."

I swallowed. If they were words meant to scare me, they worked. If they were words meant to keep me with her on the island, well, they were making their case admirably.

But I had to know.

It was like one thought was chasing the other one around the walls of my Mystis. One thought had to know what was down there. What Xander needed me for. Why Nurmedov had unfinished business with Ozmander. Who this Ozmander was. And why was the Pryystys of Thanem, Gyyd of the Woven Worlds, was so Hex bent on meting out the fate of Ozmander?

Whoever this Ozmander was, he sure was popular. I wondered why.

There was an urge to figure it all out like it was one of Bayh's arithmetic problems no one else could solve but me, but I was being chased by the fear that it would all be too much for me. That my heart would burst to see what was down there. That I was incompetent and unqualified. That I would never amount to anything. That I couldn't change the world. No, that hope was just an illusion.

Some kind of drug.

And the more steps I took down the long passageway, the further these thoughts distanced themselves from each other. But I had a feeling there would be a moment when they would collide and I'd be imprisoned by their struggle.

If that *moment* was one worthy of SanctusCraft, I had yet to see.

A bit of walking took us to a giant atrium, carved much like the inside of the sun cult temple. It was a perfect sphere with staircases running off in different directions.

"Now that's more like it." Nurmedov said.

Strangely, though, the connection ran deeper with me. It was just like I had said, like I imagined.

In a moment of CovenCraft, I was a sphere inside of a pyramid inside of a cube inside of an octahedron inside of...

I rubbed my forehead. One small point connected to infinity. It was too much to think about so I didn't.

"We cannot go just yet." Shmaila said and led us east. There were more torches and the tiles were all the color of fresh heavy cream. The passageway hooked and then opened to a series of connected dwelling chambers. I saw cushions and pots and books and even a lute. There were plants and bowls of water and places to sit. It even smelled good. Like lavender.

"I am the keeper of the gate." Shmaila said to me as Nurmedov fed the dragons right outside the entrance and everyone sat down for a moment to rest. "Which means I have to prepare everyone properly before they go and minister to their every need if and when they come back."

There was a coo in her voice that made me think this was one of her favorite things to do.

I followed her past a few chambers into one full of chests and crates. They were made of marred and nicked wood. Dark and storied. The brass hinges and clasps were greening with age.

"Now, lets see…" Shmalia tapped a few and then threw one open. "Ah yes…"

She pulled out several things and handed them to me. She kept on going till my hands were full and I thought I would fall over.

The pants and tunic were a soft but durable material, olive colored. There was a leather jerkin and a tight-fitting vest of gold and silver scales. The boots were dark like the chest that held them, as was the wide belt with its fat silver buckle.

Shmaila didn't stop there. She gave me a cape and a pointed helm.

"Wash up and change." She said. "And I'll be right back."

She was gone in a breath and I looked around at all the chests, wondering how many had gone before me and how many would go after.

Why? For what purpose?

I pondered all that as I bathed. Each chamber had a very small antechamber with a stall and a drain. The water, in small pots, was cold but it smelled slightly of lemon and made throwing the new clothes and things on my body feel right somehow.

Like I was ready. Finally.

Shmaila returned when I slipped the helm on. It had no facial protection but had a net of gold and silver scales cascading down the back like hair.

"Here, let me help." She said and wrapped the cape around me. It was a dark green velvet, like old growth trees in the deep forest.

I felt cozy inside with her hands on my shoulders, with the care in which she had prepared me. I had no thoughts of fear, or of adventure. Just that she cherished me. It was tangible inside, like some sort of food I had eaten. Her presence was nourishing. Her words gave me strength.

"I have one more thing for you." She said and held an amulet in her hand. "This is mine. It will protect you from...things."

"Things?" I asked as I took it, unsurely.

"Things I cannot describe. Things which the senses cannot grasp, only things your Sanctus can perceive."

"Oh." I said, knowing what she meant.

The amulet would ensure my connection to SanctusCraft would remain, lest something tried to block it.

Or break it.

She placed the amulet around my neck and tucked it behind my armored vest. It looked just like a piece of old wood upon a cord of leather but I didn't question what it was. It felt warm against my skin, close to my heart.

"I know you will not stay." Shmaila said, her lips fat and pouty, slowly spreading into a smile. "But do not forget me. You have a home here, always. I will teach you things no one else knows, and I will show you things no one else has ever seen."

Then she kissed me on each cheek and told me it was time to go.

THIRTY

Xander was off in the corner, pondering a long scroll when I joined the group again in the entrance chamber. Nurmedov was eating a salad of potatoes, carrots, smoked trout, onions, and something deliciously creamy looking. We had all bathed but Ilan and I were the only ones who had changed clothes. Ilan took my breath away for a moment, and I found Nurmedov staring at me as he sat on a cushion, his cheeks bulging with food.

"You don't look so bad yourself."

I pushed him in the chest as I passed him and he almost fell over. I must admit, I didn't know how I looked, but I felt good. I felt lighter, quicker, and as if I was fully engaged in what was going on. Like I could see every little tile in the room and could smell every grain of salt on the potatoes Nurmedov was eating.

I stood before Ilan as he stood before me. There was a hardness set into his eyes and a fierceness gained by the new armor he wore. It looked as if it was made of liquid silver, poured out upon him to cover him from head to toe. It caught every ray of candle flame and bent it across the chiseled shape of his body, as if little sprites were constantly darting through his suit.

Every remnant of him being a Paladyr was gone, save the rune sword.

The ash shield was gone, too, replaced by one of hammered metal and jewels that looked like a lion's face, the eyes inset with bloody garnets.

"There's no turning back." He said.

I gave him a hug, which rewarded us with an awkward *clank.*

"Together again." I whispered in his ear, and he smiled hollowly as we all left the dwelling chambers and followed Shmaila into the giant spherical chamber in the center of the pyramid.

Xander spoke up as we hit the staircase winding down around the sphere to its base.

"So the mountain is a perfect mirror." He told me. "It has gates above as well as beneath."

That made sense why the top was lost in the clouds, an icy glacier like diamonds at its peak.

I chanced a gaze up the sphere and would've lost my balance had Nurmedov not snagged my arm and brought me back.

"None of that now." He said. "Eyes ahead."

I nodded, hearing the warning again in his voice. *Don't trust him.*

I swallowed as we descended.

This was only the beginning.

"It's okay." He whispered, hands on my shoulders. "Just stick close to me."

I nodded and the steps ended. Even behind us, the dragons, keeping along the wall, were well aware of what was going on. Their steps were soft, nearly too soft to be heard, save the click of their claws on the stone.

The staircase continued winding to the bottom of the sphere till we'd left it entirely, and the staircase became straight before us, boxed in by smooth slate walls, slanting downward at a steep angle, beginning wide and narrowing with each step till we were single file.

Shmaila lit the way with her wand, and the path ended when we came to an old door, plastered with runes and dried blood. Smeared, like a desperate hand had been responsible.

I snuck a peek at it past Ilan's lion shield and wished I hadn't. I wondered about the dried blood. It made me shiver.

Shmaila stared at it for a moment and then said something like *hmm* and waved her wand over it. The door slid open without a sound and we continued into what I saw was a massive cavern lake.

The shoreline was a narrow and uneven band of pebbles and I watched in awe as Shmaila shed her cape and dropped her lit wand on top of it and dove into the water.

It was thick and black and oily and ate her up without so much as a splash.

Something like silence filled our ears for several heartbeats and then there was a *plunk* and the grinding of stone gears. It was an awful sound that made my bones feel weak within my skin. I stifled a gasp as the waterline began to recede.

Rows and rows of eroded pillars were revealed at the draining of the lake, and at the very end of them, deep down within the lumpy bowl of slick stone, Shmaila stood before a gate of glistening onyx.

Again, I shivered.

I was not ready for this.

Still we waited at the shoreline till the lake had completely drained. It was absolutely giant. It made me truly wonder at the world beneath my feet as I never had before. One cannot know what's beneath the surface of the earth till they put one foot in front of the other and find out.

Xander collected her cape and wand and set off down into the slick bowl of the drained lake. I squinted as he passed by the ruined pillars, their half-broken grandeur making the whole thing so surreal.

How could I not trust a man that so casually strode straight into the abyss?

Watching him walk sent my shivers running the other way and filled me with a warmth that I could not describe and I pushed past Nurmedov to follow him.

The stone of the basin was slick underfoot but my well-made boots saw me safely past the looming pillars, some sheared off like broken old teeth, some still stretching to what would've been the waterline.

As I walked and felt the age of the place, and wondered at the ages of what this journey would lay before my eyes. And why me, of all people, had to be the one to stay with Xander, to bring him back.

Wasn't there someone else?

Shmaila stood before the sealed gate. Its size was hidden in the lack of light, but it felt larger than the gate to Kalazaris. The onyx glistened in a dark and hungry way and I stood next to Xander as Shmaila looked him in the eye.

"You sure this is what you want?"

He only nodded and she turned to the gate, her gaze lingering on mine for a moment.

And as the rest of our party passed by the pillars behind us, Shmaila said ten words in a language I had never heard before and that sound of stone gnawing against stone that turned my bones to liquid and my courage to ash pushed the gates of the abyss wide open like an unseen hand.

THIRTY-ONE

The dragons fell from the sky like stones.

If you could call it a sky.

It was more like a dome, a curved skin of dead earth and darkness, and we rapidly sank beneath it.

We had entered this new world from the very top, this realm beneath our own, and instead of taking the long journey zigzagging down the pyramid mountain, the perfect mirror of the surface, we simply hopped on the backs of our dragons and followed Xander and Nilius through the murk.

The gray skin of the ceiling faded away as the endless landscape of dark shadows and dust spread before us.

Vast plains of nothingness sat between shoulders of stone, bluffs and cliffs, the bases of which were stacked with the bones of those who'd fallen off the edge.

Wide basins captured small ponds of black tar and tangled thorns clung to the shore. Death gray dust and ashes and sand covered the ground like flour on a baker's board, or snow upon the highroad. The bones of prehistory curled upon the ground, half-embedded in it. Bleached spines and limbs, frozen in time.

At times, giant chasms opened up as if a massive pair of claws had torn through the landscape. They were jagged, uneven, and of no certain depth.

My eyes lingered as we glided through the heavy, stagnant air.

There was no light. No, nothing that even resembled the deep burning darkness of the black night sun.

But still we could see, as if the whole of the abyss was glazed in an eerie luminescence that came from the many Sanctuses of all those who had fallen to their deaths in this bitter land.

We flew for hours, wandering through this stark and dead terrain, all of it looking the same, maddeningly so. Were we going in circles? Certainly not. Xander knew where he was going.

Didn't he?

The wandering and wondering continued for hours more. Or maybe not. Maybe they were only minutes that seemed like hours, stretched out and hammered into my Mystis by the unchanging terrain. By the deafness of it all.

I fought the madness creeping in. I knew as sure as I knew there was still breath in my body that it would only get worse.

Madness.

We finally settled on a canyon floor the size of a thousand cities. The canyon walls, dark slate bruised blue by the strange illumination, faded into obscurity at the edges of the horizon. Again, I wallowed in the size of the place...the secrets it held. The sheer depth of the unknown. Millions of moments, lost in the unseen expanse.

I felt so small. So weak. So helpless.

Nurmedov hopped off his dragon and grumbled to me as he walked by.

"He's lost."

Xander had taken two steps from Nilius and was peering out into the waste as Nurmedov approached.

"So X doesn't mark the spot, huh?"

Xander only grimaced at the adventurer and returned to divine the distance. To what? To whatever he'd come down here for. I still didn't know. I didn't think he was ever going to tell me. Nurmedov didn't tell me, so he didn't know either.

He'd told me not to trust Xander, which meant he didn't either. Or did he? And he just wanted *me* not to trust him.

"You're lost." Nurmedov said.

"No, I'm not."

"Can't you admit when you're wrong?"

Xander sighed. He tipped his chin to the smaller man and squinted. "Trying to find your way is not the same as trying to find someone."

"Why not? They're one in the same for you." Nurmedov scoffed and walked back, playing with the handle of one of his daggers.

"He's not lost." He mumbled as he passed me.

I sighed and sat up in the saddle. Nearly at the same moment, Daisey decided, since we were done flying for more than two minutes, that it was time to rest and plopped down on her side.

And threw me from the saddle.

I hit the ground and rolled ungracefully, my helmet rattling off into the dust.

Nurmedov was over to me in a moment and helped me up.

"You okay?" He said.

"I'm f..." I was about to say *fine* but a sharp pain ran through my back and I hissed. "Nope."

"Great..." He said again, sarcasm heavy on his tongue, and as he passed me he reached down to snatch up my helmet.

It didn't take The Learnyd to see how frustrated he was.

He handed back my helmet with a forced smile. I wondered if he had something to say. His mouth looked strained he was trying so hard to keep it shut.

He turned to leave and I placed my hand on his shoulder.

"What?" He said, flatly.

"Nurmedov, I know it's really hard for you to not see the sun for so long…but we'll be out of here before you know it."

Nurmedov blinked a few times and stared at me, his eyes glazed.

"How'd you know?"

I tapped his shoulder.

"I could feel it." I said, squeezing his shoulder. "You love the sun. You need it. Without the sun, what are you?"

He flashed me a crooked smile.

"Just another incurable."

I nodded and he left with a spring in his step.

Xander seemed to find what he was looking for, maybe some scent on a wind that didn't blow or some dust mote that spoke to him in a language only he knew. Or a path he'd taken before and carefully marked. Forgotten, to finally recall.

I woke Daisey up and she shook the dust off her coat. Her long, gray beard curled at her feet. I had to cover my eyes from the cloud that drifted my way like a ghost. I sighed to see how my fine clothes were already ruined with remnants of the abyss.

Death was already clinging to me. The ashes and bones of the fallen, ageless and lost.

And as I pulled myself up in the saddle and we took to the air again, I couldn't help but think about Nurmedov.

Because he was a man of the sun cult, and missed that luminous star that gave heat and light and color to all living things.

But that was the only reason I knew. Because I missed the sun, too. I felt like something had been stolen from me.

Not because I felt as much when I touched him.

To be honest, I couldn't feel anything. It was like everything beneath the dome was dead.

Echoless. Lost. Silenced. I couldn't feel anything.

Not even the talisman around my neck that was supposed to seal my connection to SanctusCraft.
Nothing.

THIRTY-TWO

We flew and flew and it all looked the same. Captive, in the saddle, I was beginning to gather more than a bit of Nurmedov's frustration myself. Xander knew what he was doing, didn't he? It seemed like he wasn't telling anyone, so if anyone knew, it would have to be him. Who knows, maybe he'd lost it, and things didn't add up like he thought they would. Maybe he'd planned it all out beneath the sanity of the orange midday sun, only to find it was unraveling before his eyes down here in the wasteland of the lost and the forgotten. Life had a way of making one hope something one moment and then stealing it the next. Maybe his grand schemes were failing under the mockery of this immense nothingness. Telling him there was nothing for him here. Nothing for any of us. It was all a waste.

And so we just kept flying around, like we were on some demented circuit. Passing slump-shouldered cliffs and dusty basins. All alone with the heavy, stagnant air and the even duller gnaw of our own thoughts.

Until a giant chasm spread open before us like a great yawning mouth.

Fear swelled in the pit of my stomach just to see it. To gaze upon the bitter black scar ripped open and running freely across the ground. Glowing with an unearthly darkness. Knowing we were headed straight for it. My limbs tensed up to resist. But there was no resistance. There was only momentum.

Unstoppable momentum.

It was the spot Xander had been looking for. Or had it been looking for us? Calling to us…waiting for us to fall into its stomach of silent stones to be forever sealed.

I shuddered.

Xander spun Nilius into a sharp turn and disappeared down into the jet black vent, cut deep within the skin of dust and decay.

Daisey followed lazily, her bulk plummeting us both down into the darkness. Suddenly all the endlessness around me, the deserts of dead cliffs and parched wastes disappeared. Terror no long wandered aimlessly in the basins, but clamped down on my shoulders like wolves' teeth.

Diving into the black vent was like passing through a veil. Immediately the cold hit me and shocked me and stabbed my lungs with frozen fangs.

But there was no turning back. The vent fell and fell and fell and the dragons nimbly avoided sharp tooth-like shelves and shorn granite faces reaching out like hands to swipe us from our saddles.

I gripped the reins so tight my knuckles turned white and I pressed myself down in the saddle, narrowing my teary eyes to slits as the vent twisted and turned and spun lower and lower into the earth. Every gasp for breath seemed to push equilibrium further and further away from me, like I was chasing a memory.

I never thought I'd long for the dust and cliffs of the deserts above us.

But the plummeting would not stop. We just kept falling and falling. And falling.

And falling.

Blackness seeped into the edges of my vision, and I felt myself become sick. The sensation of my stomach being in my throat would not leave, and the tissue between my ears seemed to scramble.

My mouth stretched open, searching for a clean breath, or a scream, and I swooned in the saddle, falling face-first into Daisey's soft black fur.

THIRTY-THREE

The wind kissed my face with a soft caress before a vicious howl tore through my bones and woke me up with a jolt.

"Hey, it's okay. It's okay." Ilan said, hugging me and holding me in the crook of his elbow. "Take it easy, you're okay."

Startled, I could only see his face, his clear blue eyes and the hardness in them, the firmness of his jaw, and the hunger in his silver armor, sucking up all the light there was.

But even his nearness could not rip the sensation from me.

Abandonment.

Wild and untamed, like a fire in the forest, the tangible sense of being left and lost and forgotten and abandoned forever echoed through my Sanctus like thunder on the plains.

I hugged Ilan back, tightly, and inhaled the musty smell of his sweat, and the cold tang of his armor. I held on to him as he held on to me. He was not a ghost. He was as real as I was.

As real as the feelings were.

I shuddered.

"Hungry?" It was Nurmedov, on his haunches to my right. I turned, sharply, still surprised to hear voices and see faces at all when I still felt the lingering effects of having my Sanctus stripped from me.

I tapped my chest frantically. The talisman. It was still there.

Still there...then why had it been so real? For a breath...a moment. All ripped away and severed. Cut off...

I dug my palms into my eyes and groaned.

"Hey, Rosalyn, you hungry?" Nurmedov repeated again.

I shook my head, licking my lips. They were chapped and bumpy.

"You can have my sandwich." I said.

"Thanks!" He smiled and went back to the saddlebags that contained the day's ration of cheese and bread. He seemed cheered up with each bite.

As I gained my legs again and felt the world wobble, I determined the only Craft Nurmedov cared about was one concerning food. Surely there was a Craft for that.

I think the only way to kill Nurmedov was to take away his food. No wonder he'd survived so many adventures. The man simply ate his way through any exploit. It gave new meaning to the phrase *leaving a trail of breadcrumbs.*

"Where are we?" I asked, my voice sounding as weak as I felt. When there was no answer I pressed past Ilan's lingering embrace of hard muscle and cold armor to see for myself.

We stood on the meager shoreline of a black horizon, fading in tones of darkness as it bent into the void of infinity.

To see it was to see the black and gluey sap of nightmares, the wet opus of oblivion.

"The Sea of the Dead." Xander said, as he stood on the shore, staring out into the many colors of eternal darkness.

"And no gulls!" Nurmedov laughed as he ate his sandwich peacefully.

Ilan snorted at him and took my hand.

"You sure you're okay?"

"She's fine." Xander spoke, his gaze staid and stoic. His voice, too, had fallen to a monotone.

I gathered that we were closer than ever to whatever he sought.

I took two steps toward him, still finding my legs. I felt as if I had been turned inside out, as if a dream had been my reality, and now my reality was a dream.

But those feelings were mocked by the gravity of what stretched before me. By the heaviness of the atmosphere. The silence. The chill. The color. The Sea itself.

And the cursed permanency of the whole thing. It sat in my mouth like poison.

My steps took me the shore's edge and Xander grabbed my arm.

"No further." He said. A warning. Then, he added, "We wait."

"For what?" I asked.

"Crossing."

My eyebrows slid up my forehead.

"We're going to *cross* the Sea of The Dead? Don't you...I don't know, have to be dead to do that?"

Xander grimaced. His voice was barely audible, his face shadowed by the Sea.

"You know so much, yet still fail to see." He said. "When the time comes, do not close your eyes. All will be revealed and the choice will be yours and yours alone. You will touch the past and the future one in the same just as it will touch you and you will be forever changed. Your choice will mark your days forever, and the days of those yet to come. You will see the truth for what it is, and will carry the sword that it is all your days, until your feet have tread every corner of the Woven Worlds and your breath is no more within you. But only if you believe. Only if you believe there is more to see than you see with your eyes. Do not close them, but do not see with them alone. Heed my words and many shall live. Heed not and many shall die."

Xander walked off down the shore, leaving me to stare after him, feeling numb.

I could hear Nurmedov munching on my sandwich and turned to him to find him staring at me.

"What?"

"Aren't you going to write that down?"

I smirked and plopped down next to him with a sigh. I guess Daisey was wearing off on me. Riders must take after their dragons. I wanted to stop and sleep and felt heavy and weary. I let my head fall in my palms and rubbed my eyes with the heels of my hands.

"Why?"

"Because that was a prophecy."

"I got it, Nurmedov, thanks."

"I got one for you too."

"Oh yeah?"

"Befriend a man with bread, and he will lend you daggers."

"Um...thanks, but that's not a prophecy."

"No?"

"No, that would be a proverb. If it even is one."

"You doubting my wisdom, Rosalyn?"

I frowned.

"How could I ever do such a thing?"

"All I'm saying is," He popped the last of the crusty bread into his mouth and brushed his hands together, and then on his trousers. "When we cross the Sea, there's no telling what will happen. But I've got three daggers to watch your back."

Nurmedov leaned in so close I could smell the nutty cheese on his breath.

"And one dagger to plunge into his."

THIRTY-FOUR

The roar ripped across the waters before I could ask whose back he was talking about. Shady Xander or this elusive Ozmander or maybe even Ilan or someone else.

It was a hollow thunder, a dry and sucking storm of rage. Bristling and crackling like wildfire run amok.

"What was that?"

Nurmedov stood up and peered into the darkness. I stood up, too, not comfortable anymore to sit along the shore.

"Leviathan."

I swallowed and turned to face him.

"Who?"

"A sea-serpent the size of a large city who feeds on the pride of the dead. On vanity, greed, lust and conceit. Because those things don't go away, you know. Legacies live on. They survive like starlight and stones."

I wondered at that. Everyone could leave an impact on the Woven Worlds somehow. Everyone did. Whatever they did had an affect, just like Shmaila had said. The Woven Worlds responded to the actions of those who shaped them.

"The Sea of The Dead is his to roam." Nurmedov continued. "He's well fed from all the souls lost here. From all the charred remains of humanity. The memories."

The roar rose up again, a distant thing that sounded like a tornado unleashed from the jaws of a volcano.

"There is not a more fearless beast in all of the Woven Worlds. Good steel swords are like blades of grass to him. His heart is harder than a black diamond. His eyes are made of lightning and his mouth is a cauldron of flames."

I shuddered as the roar faded, the very sound of it slithering in echoes throughout the darkness. I imagined massive coils of armored flesh, and a face that would stop the heart of the bravest warrior just to behold it.

"You've...seen him before?" I asked. There was a quaver in my voice.

"Yes I have." Nurmedov nodded grimly. "It was years ago. Though...one doesn't soon forget those kinds of things."

"We won't be fighting him, will we?"

"I sure hope not!" Nurmedov chuckled, resting his fingers on the handle of one of his daggers. The amber one, by the looks of it. "No, the only way across the Sea is without him knowing about it."

"How do you..."

"So many questions." Xander said and spooked me. I turned around and put my hand to my chest, catching my breath.

"Can you stop doing that?"

Xander would never stop sneaking up on people. His grimace said as much. It must've been one of the small pleasures of his life, to sneak up on people. I sighed, knowing he wouldn't apologize.

"Watch and learn." He said.

Xander turned to the Sea, inhaled and exhaled. He stilled himself, till he was calm as the water upon which he gazed without blinking.

Then, he knelt ever so slowly and held his hands just above the water and closed his eyes.

Ilan came up behind me to watch. I could smell his armor. Like fresh frost and harder than a long winter. Perhaps he wanted a piece of this Leviathan creature, but he was obviously captivated by the CovenCraft he was forced to hate as a Palaydr.

But weren't we always enamored with the things we were told we couldn't do?

And Ilan, forced to hunt those who had made CovenCraft their lives, didn't that mean he'd studied it and become consumed by it? By the mystical fascination that it was?

All of our eyes were on the water as it began to move.

At first, they were little bubbles, rising to pop on the surface. Xander lowered his chin and sighed, his hands quivering in the slightest as he slowed his breathing even more, so that he barely drew breath at all.

The bubbles increased, as did small spots of foam, rising from the depths of the Sea. The bubbles were dark like dead waters themselves, but the foam was a grayish color, like liquid ash.

The roar shook our bones and Xander didn't even flinch. It seemed closer than last time, perhaps that was the nature of the echo, and whatever wind there was, like the wind that had awoken me.

The wind that Leviathan created when he coiled his massive bulk and splashed across the surface of the waves. Or when he roared, screaming his hatred for all living things with the voice of death itself.

I bit my lip as the echoes of the roar died in our ears and the bubbles increased.

Xander's face was pale and his hands were spidery with veins.

But the bubbles didn't stop. They grew in number, rapidly collecting and coalescing until the foam itself began to weave its way into an organic shape.

A shape that curled and coiled across the waves, bending and shifting and gaining form and substance.

A snake.

Ilan gripped his rune sword tight as Xander completed his work. The former Paladyr's blue eyes were wide, his lips tight.

Xander had made a snake of bubbles and foam, a spongy bridge of congealed liquids to carry us to the other side.

I didn't know which part of his CovenCraft was more astounding, but as Xander stood up and exhaled and opened his eyes, I knew his work was complete, and the mottled gray tube of squishy bubbles and foam floating in place looked just as much like a snake as it did our only way across The Sea of The Dead. It moved in the water as if it were alive, swimming on its own to keep the bridge that it was afloat and keep our feet dry from the poison waters of the Sea.

Xander proved as much by taking the first step.

"Come on," he said. "We don't have much time."

Nurmedov carried but one pack as well as his bow and arrows and nimbly hopped past Xander to begin the long and squiggly path across the Sea. Head down, his steps were sure and confident, like a wire-walker in a carnival.

"Ilan, you're next." Xander motioned with his chin. "Don't be afraid."

The former Paladyr complied, passing me a glance of awe veiled in disgust. It was a look I knew well. It was the look he always gave me when I was right.

Ilan followed closely behind Nurmedov. I swallowed the dryness in my throat as the two began to fade in the darkness, as if the shades of the abyss were eating them one step at a time.

"Rosalyn."

I looked at him. At the face that had told me so many truths and so many lies. I remember what Nurmedov said, and all my thoughts concerning those few words were bundled up in one messy cloud.

I was not taking a single step till I knew the truth.

"No." I said.

His nostrils flared and his jaw tensed but his voice was low and controlled.

"Rosalyn, there is *no* time for this."

"Tell me anyway. Why the Hex are you down here? Who are you looking for and why?"

Xander's upper lip curled.

"Rosalyn, take your first step by yourself or I'll carry you over my shoulder."

I curled my hands into fists to defy him, but nearby Leviathan roared and he didn't have to tell me to walk across the snake bridge of foam and bubbles.

I ran.

THIRTY-FIVE

The snake bridge squished and splashed but I never got wet. As fast as I ran, it moved beneath my feet and lent its body to my frantic escape. Leviathan's cataclysmic roar tore at my guts like a knife. Fear snapped at my belly, trying to make its home within me. They were jagged, angry cuts, as if the whole deafening echo of Leviathan's roar was a collection of thousands and thousands of screams. A hive of them, scattered to the wind. Rising and seeking and scratching at my skin. Digging into my ears. Clawing at my eyes. His wrath shook The Sea, and the snake bridge rose and fell as his sloshing wake let me know he wasn't far away.

I thought I saw a flash of light out of the corner of my eye, but I wouldn't dare look. I didn't want to lose my balance. It was one foot in front of the other. Step after step after step after step. The Sea heaved and swelled with the nearness of the beast, and I ran like I've never run before.

I saw Nurmedov first, the silhouette of his honeywood bow flooding me with relief. The swagger he carried, the ease with which he strode straight into the mouth of all things horrifying. Ilan was next to him, sword drawn, in case it came to that. In case a pair of jaws came for him. He would not go quietly. Xander was behind them both. He was a dark ghost upon the water. Barely even there.

Behind them? That's right, he could do that. Close the distance between two points like folding a piece of paper. I was just still getting used to it. I wanted to ask him all the things that were possible in CovenCraft but I already knew one could form worlds somehow. Whole worlds. And I could barely cross a bridge.

But thank heavens it was running out. I could barely breath. I was a walker, not a runner. I could walk the whole day straight but I couldn't run to save my life. And here I was. Clean shoreline of dusty gray grass and pale dirt lay ahead of me.

Ten strides...seven...five...three...

The ground inverted itself as I rose in the air. I lost myself in the space of a moment, not knowing which direction I had been thrown. The crash followed. The explosion of thousands of feet of armored flesh and dead water. The squelch of Xander's bridge of bubbles and foam being ripped and torn to shreds in the jaws of Leviathan.

The ground punched me hard, and I lost my helmet again, tangling myself in the cape that was no longer emerald green and a Tempus that was no longer lusting for adventure. The pain in my back throbbed and something in my ankle did too. I hissed as I was rolled over by helping hands, and unwrapped from my tangled cape like a birthday gift.

"Rosy, you alright?"

It was Ilan. Ilan who somehow looked scared and invincible in the same breath. Ilan who pulled me up and dusted me off and stuck my helmet back on my head.

"Now you know why I like to keep a low profile in the sun cult temple." Nurmedov smirked as he walked past, hitching up his pack. "They have really good garlic bread, too."

Xander was close behind and motioned for Ilan to follow Nurmedov, since he knew the way.

I rubbed my sore jaw, which didn't quite feel like it did before the crossing. I think it'd been my own knee that'd smacked me. Thank the stars I hadn't bit my tongue.

Xander was cloaked in darkness for a moment, looking back, and then took me by the elbow and guided me forward in a quick walk.

"Don't ever do that again." He said.

"I don't plan on ever being back here again to try it."

Xander's cheeks pulsed and he sighed as we put distance between ourselves and the shore. Leviathan roared once more and I saw the wind of it brush through the gray, straw-like grass as it sat scruffy and dead on the pale sand. Leviathan thrashed in the water and splashed out into a new direction, distracted by something to eat. Seeking something else to terrorize. To feed the formless hunger that he was.

We had escaped his eyes of lighting and mouth of cauldron flame.

But I hadn't escaped my need to know why Xander was here and what he was doing.

And we weren't far from the moment of truth.

The eerie shapes of a ruined temple rising up from the earth confirmed as much.

THIRTY-SIX

The temple was scattered across the space of a massive crater, making the whole thing appear as if it'd fallen straight from the stars and broken apart upon impact.

Perhaps it had.

Surrounded by wayward dunes and darkness, it was a ghost of stony angles and spires, dominated by rows upon rows of obelisks that led the way to one large pyramid, the top of which was obscured in darkness.

Several small outbuildings spread around in organic shapes like creeper vines and roots, some of them nearly fully submerged in the pale sand. One could think, with the violence in which they were embedded in the landscape, that a tremendous whirlwind had been unleashed from the pyramid, even further destroying the already desolate land.

And however the eye scraped across it, the path of obelisks leading straight to the large pyramid dominated perception, sticking up defiant and perfect and ominous in the ravaged waste.

I knew no other way to describe it. It was as if fear had a home and I was walking straight into it. As if the loneliness and abandonment I had felt when I had come to my senses on the shoreline were fear's own children, and they had been raised here. Cultivated and nurtured and fed all the lies that had become their truths. Here they had grown strong. Indomitable.

Invincible.

Here, they had learned to become the weapons that could destroy empires without even firing a single arrow.

I closed my eyes as the coarse sand mushed under my every step, and the straw-like grass made scratchy hisses as remnants of Leviathan's roar still rippled across the land.

Here, walking straight into fear's own lair, I was scared out of my mind. Scared numb. I couldn't even feel my own breath. I was heading straight into the temple like a nightwalker. Pulled into its own dark heart the way an apple fell from a tree, or a star shot across the sky. Possessed by momentum not my own.

Tears slid down my face. Silent tears. Deaf tears. I never knew a human soul could feel so alone even when someone was walking right beside them, step for step.

"Will it help?" Xander asked as we neared the unmarked entrance to the eerie skeleton that was the temple. His voice was soft and pulled me from my thoughts.

"What?"

"If I tell you the whole story, will it help?"

I combed my hair behind my ears and crossed my arms.

"I'm here...for you." I said. "To help bring you back. Like you asked. Would it be better if I finally knew what you as of yet haven't wanted to tell me and more than likely still don't?"

Xander looked down his nose at me. I was used to it by now, but I could never stop that initial jab of a feeling that he carried so much scorn in his Sanctus towards me.

Towards human life.

"Rosalyn, you hold something very precious within you, and I've tried so hard to distance myself from you so I don't jeopardize it."

I found my breath shallow within me.

"What?"

"I feel..." Xander squinted as he peered out into the limitless dunes, shaped by the years of Leviathan's roar. By a million empty echoes. "Even to name it would be to jeopardize its purity. Of all the secrets I keep, I would keep that one still."

I walked closer to him and said nothing. I didn't know what to say. I was too numb to smile, and my tears dried on my cheeks. Ahead of us, Nurmedov was pointing out certain features of the temple to Ilan, who was taking it all in with a hunter's eyes. His sword was sheathed, but he was ready for conflict as sure as there was breath in his body.

"If you don't want to tell me why you came down here, that's okay. If you don't want to tell me what's special about me, it's okay." I found myself saying between sniffs. "In my short life I've had everyone else telling me what they think I am instead of letting me be what I want. I came down here with you because I wanted to. I was old enough to walk the Nomyd Path alone and maybe I'm still walking it. I don't know. Maybe I never stopped trying to see if you're okay after that first moment I saw a body half-buried in the snow. Maybe I don't know what it means to be a Nomyd and roam the earth seeking to help people and I just care too much about the first person I happened to see that needed me. Maybe it's none of that and I don't even know why I came down here with you, but I don't think we always have to know why we do something in order to do it." I smiled a vacant thing. "At least I want to be able to live my life that way. I don't want to have to know everything. I don't want to have to understand something before I believe it."

"Hmm." Xander said, and then added. "I think you'll know why after it's all over."

Something sickening crossed his face and he half-turned as he said it. For a moment I thought of a creature under the surface of the water. A tail flickering away in the murk. To try and see it was to send it skittering away.

Some creatures refused to be seen.

We continued walking as the husks of the old outbuildings swelled around us like bleached and lidless eyes. Watching us. Watching all. Seeing nothing. Blind to the pain of the silent hell of the abyss. Hey, maybe I hadn't seen anything at all. I might've imagined the anguish I saw in him, the living torture that it was. As deep as the chasm we'd fallen into to get down here. As raw and hungry as the ten thousand roars that shaped this place.

Or maybe it was shadow. Maybe there was no light here but the light we carried inside.

And the darkness, too.

THIRTY-SEVEN

Step by step we entered the crater. The change in height was subtle, as if we were ever so slowly sinking. Submerging ourselves in another realm. An invisible sphere. An altered state. I couldn't fight the fear that came from it. I reached out for Xander's arm and squeezed tight. I felt the blood pumping through his black leather tunic. If it was fear or adrenaline in anticipation of the fight to come, I couldn't know. Nothing in my Mystis was straight. It was scattered. Windblown like the outbuildings surrounding the perfect rows of obelisks and their arrow-like path to the giant pyramid.

And the change in atmosphere? That was not so subtle. Passing the line in the sand that separated the temple from the rest of the waste, we were blasted with icy air. I squinted just to fight the sting as it jabbed frozen daggers into my eyes. Angry as it was, seeking us out, there was no wind that drove it. It was like kitchen duty at Bayh on the day of onion stew. There was no escape from it. Hatred was in it, a whisper just on the edge of hearing. The echoes of a corrupted Sanctus, ever fermenting and permeating the realm of the crater temple. As we walked and our eyes drifted across the scattered outbuildings, I realized the paleness of them was not only from whatever stone was used to construct them, but also from frost. It was horrible. I wondered if I'd ever get to the temple or be frozen alive in the process.

Fear slithered along the ground like a thousand unseen snakes and I bit my lip as Nurmedov stopped walking and peered into the darkness at the top of the pyramid.

"What?" Ilan said as we all came to a halt.

There was something hard in Nurmedov's face. Nurmedov who could see the silver lining in a shipwreck. Nurmedov who could slice the mold off of a loaf of bread two weeks old with one of his daggers, pop it in his mouth, and say it tasted a bit nutty.

Nurmedov who was only here to settle a score as old as his own life.

"Hmm…" He said, licking his lips and wiping his brow. "Maybe nothing." He turned to me and threw me a causal smile. "One can start to see things down here. One can go a bit meshuggah, you know."

Xander said nothing and probed the dead space of the silent temple. Stretching out his Sanctus to find something. To find someone.

"Hey," Nurmedov came closer. "He didn't tell you why we're here, did he?"

I shook my head and shivered.

"Well let me tell you why *I'm* here."

"This is no time for a story." Xander warned.

"Save it old man." Nurmedov growled. "The girl's got a right to hear me out." He looked back to me and smiled. "Besides, I love to hear myself talk, remember?"

Xander threw Nurmedov a menacing glance and behind Nurmedov, Ilan tensed, although it didn't take The Learnyd to feel combat in the air.

It was coming. It had been coming for a lifetime longer than my own. Building. Aching for blood. Seeking it out with swords only growing sharper by time's own whetstone.

I wallowed in the weakness and deafness I felt. The helplessness as one pledged to help others. To heal.

Blood would be spilt this day and there was nothing I could do to stop it.

When Xander remained stoic, Nurmedov nodded slowly and turned his eyes to me. They were icier than ever, as if they were finally at home in the frigid atmosphere of the temple. Or the frost was feeding something primal in his Mystis, and it was taking him over, like a virus.

"Once upon a time, there was a world within the Woven Worlds where time stood still. Ageless begat ageless. Beauty was both King and Queen and the sun itself was alive in the heart of every living soul. Ask me what happened."

My voice was a peep. I knew where it was going, but I didn't have the heart to say.

"What happened?"

"Ozmander happened."

"Ozmander?" Ilan piped up. "That's what this is all about?"

He walked off in a circle and groaned, bending in half till he sank to the ground on his haunches. His hard cheeks and chin were strained as he stared up at the pyramid and then shook his head.

"Wh...who's Ozmander?" I said, suddenly more scared than I'd ever been.

"Good question, Rosalyn." Nurmedov smiled, wild and insane. "Ozmander was a traveller from another world. A seeker of wisdom. An angel of light. He came to this storied world of agelessness and beauty, of immortality and ten thousand endless summers..."

Nurmedov trailed off, his eyes drifting around, searching his thoughts. His memories.

"And..."

"And what do you think?" Nurmedov snapped. "Ozmander brought winter to freeze the sun. He brought war to deface the beauty. He brought death to end life. But worse than that, he brought his corrupt magicks and took every good thing that world had to offer and sucked it up for himself."

My mouth sagged as the cold and numbness possessed me.

"You see, Rosalyn, Ozmander came to seek wisdom. A searcher of hidden truths. But he tricked that world and every living thing in it into revealing those sacred truths to him so he could use them against that very same world. Against *all* of the Woven Worlds."

"What...what did he do?"

It was Ilan who answered.

"He destroyed that world. He devoured it. Like Nurmedov in a bakery. And then he moved on."

The thought paralyzed me. The thought of all life, sucked up and sponged and mopped up and consumed.

But no tears would come.

It was as if there was nothing tangible to connect to, in memorandum, nothing to touch.

There was no sorrow because there was nothing.

The world was gone. Devoured by Ozmander.

And *nothing* remained.

"And so he moved on," Ilan said, "Coming to another world to devour them too."

"But the world fought back." Nurmedov said, his chest swelling with pride. "For they knew how to live in constant unrest and distrust. They knew how to hunt and fight and carve out their own survival as the world itself warred with those who walked its own surface for supremacy."

"Wrong world to show up to." Ilan muttered darkly.

"Sure was." Nurmedov said.

"Because it was *this* one." I mumbled, my eyes downcast. "It was *our* world."

"Sure was." Nurmedov nodded, toying with the handle of one of his daggers. The blood ruby one. "And before you were born, Rosalyn, there was a great war. All the Kings and Queens of this world in which we live sent their war machines and their horses and riders and all the steel in their castles to fight him."

"Him?" I squeaked. "...*just* him?"

"That's right." Ilan said. "That's how powerful Ozmander was."

I gulped my fears and shivered.

"How do you know this?" I asked Ilan.

"The Infernium. Why do you think it was created?" He muttered. "In the Ozmander war, CovenCraft was out of control. It was...it..." he shook his head as he covered his face with his hand. "I wasn't there...I just heard the stories. It's the history of the Order. Madness. It made me sick every night to read about it...like it was the war Ozmander brought that ruined CovenCraft itself. Like everything was fine and then he showed up and ruined it all."

"No, you weren't there." Nurmedov said, "but I was. I was there with my four brothers and all the other brave men from our land, sent by our beloved Matriarch, Khurshid the Great, to save our own world from this world-eating monster masquerading as a man. For, we may, as a people, be at odds with it, striving for life, but we sure as Hex don't want anyone devouring it and us along with it."

The moment he said that, it was as if the cold and dead space around us fell away, and it was only Nurmedov and I. I could not take my eyes off of his icy gaze as he recounted his tale. It made me realize *why* he could carry so much weight on his back.

What was a couple hundred pounds of food, weapons, and clothing in comparison to the weight of the world on his shoulders?

"I was old enough to fight but I was still just a young boy." He continued. "We travelled for days and days. I thought I'd never see home again. I'd never see the face of our beloved Matriarch, or the beautiful sun in the sky. And then, finally, when we met him, we realized how wrong we were to have marched against him."

Nurmedov blinked himself back to the moment and inhaled slowly, closing his eyes as he did.

"Oh how good it feels to be back."

I put my hand to my heart. It beat so hard that it hurt.

"What?" I gasped. "You mean...you fought Ozmander...*here*?"

His silence said it all.

Nurmedov sighed, staring at the pyramid.

"He killed everyone."

"Everyone?"

"Yeah...everyone but me. He just...walked down from the top of that pyramid like some kind of deity and blasted everyone to bits. Ripped their flesh from their bones, and turned their bones to powder. And their Sanctuses? He sucked them all up like a whirlpool in the sea. Swallowed them alive. Two hundred thousand screams silenced in the blink of an eye. Every one but mine."

I didn't even know what to say.

"Why did he leave me?" Nurmedov asked, his fingertips stroking the edges of his daggers, one at a time, rising up and down his chest as if waiting for one to speak to him, to beg to be pulled from the sheath and gripped tight. "That's a good question, Rosalyn. Why *did* he leave me? Why did he walk by, and stare deep into my eyes, and let me live? Why did he walk straight back up the top of that pyramid and disappear?"

My mouth was dry as the dust that covered this forsaken land.

"Why?" I croaked.

"I don't know." Nurmedov said, nudging his chin behind me. "Why don't you ask him?"

I turned to see Xander, standing there, stone still like one of the obelisks.

Tall. Obstinate. Mystical. Ageless.

His black eyes bore into mine. His Sanctus was stripped bare. I couldn't even believe the words that fell from my mouth like a clay pot to shatter into a thousand pieces.

"*You're* Ozmander?"

Xander said nothing. He simply flared his nostrils and inhaled deeply and sighed.

I turned back to Nurmedov. Insanity was a violent force bubbling just beneath his skin, ready to gush red-hot rage into his veins.

It was then Nurmedov nodded slowly, shifting his eyes from me to Xander and back to me, slowly selecting the black opal dagger from the sheath on his chest.

Xander refused to move as he did so. As the knife fell heavy from the sheath and dropped down to Nurmedov's waist. As his hand squeezed to a white and bloodless fist, and his entire arm flexed with the vengeance of a lifetime.

"Now you know." Xander said, and Nurmedov stepped forward.

But Ilan stopped him and Nurmedov spun, his face a mask of primal rage.

"Wait!" He said, throwing his hands out wide. "If *he's* Ozmander, then who the Hex is that?"

Ilan pointed to the top of the pyramid and the figure silently descending the steps one ominous footstep at a time.

He was a massive man, taller than Xander by at least a head. His body was a chiseled, broad-shouldered V and his legs and arms were thick and powerful. The plate armor that covered him from head to toe was as black as the opal on Nurmedov's dagger and his gauntlets, greaves, and shoulder plates were spiked with bitter-looking thorns.

And his face.

His face was a carved mask of black steel, just like his armor. An inhuman smile of hideous fangs and void-black eyes. A face that laughed at death and lived in the shadows of fear. Two wings rose from a strange rune-like symbol of stars and interwoven lines on his forehead, stretching parallel to the cruel and exaggerated line of his brow. Two horns rose from the symbol, too, and they must've been the length of my arm, curving gently until they reached their razor-sharp pinnacle.

Distantly, Leviathan roared. I took it as a heartless endorsement of this malevolence, this embodiment of death, destruction, and decay.

This spectral savage of the abyss.

The figure descended the pyramid, his shape becoming larger and larger and larger until he was nearly at the base of it, just a short dash away from us at the head of the obelisk-lined path.

"That..." Xander said with the crippling anguish I knew I would never understand. "Is my son."

THIRTY-EIGHT

Nurmedov's eyes darted between the two figures, the one he hated and the one that hated all living beings. I could feel it, deep inside my Sanctus, that overwhelming sensation that'd been hounding me since Shmaila opened the gates of the abyss.

The unfiltered hell of loneliness. Utter abandonment. The diet of isolation; fear, pain, anguish, regret, misunderstanding.

Hatred as thick and black as The Sea of The Dead.

The man I used to know as Xander only to learn I'd never really known him at all took a step, daring Nurmedov to finally do what he'd come to. Nurmedov didn't move. The silent descent of the dread knight that was Ozmander's son somehow rattled him. He was as pale as the snow. Frozen in place by the frightful aura of this black-clad warrior.

It was as if he'd eaten all of Nurmedov's courage. Or maybe it was just the terror of reliving it all over again, the moment when Ozmander obliterated the armies set against him, leaving only Nurmedov alive to claw his way, somehow, back to the surface of the earth.

As a young boy?

Ozmander read Nurmedov's face and then cast his eyes to mine.

"Now hear *my* story, Rosalyn." His voice was a monotone, stripped of all emotion.

"Don't listen to a word he says!" Nurmedov shouted, his head snapping back and forth between Ozmander and the massive warrior clad in black steel. He was drawing closer. Nurmedov's brows were creased in strain. He was thinking. Thinking he was too late.

Ozmander disregarded him.

"Rosalyn, listen to me. *Listen* to me."

Ilan's hand snuck to the hilt of his sword, but his gaze was lost in uncertainty.

He too, like me, wanted to help. To save. To protect. To heal. He'd once trained to walk the Nomyd Path. But it hadn't been good enough for him.

He had a sword. Swords caused wounds. They divided things, like families and countries. They cut off heads and pierced hearts. They rusted with age and lost their edge.

He'd wanted change bad enough to strap on the sword at The Infernium's expense, to learn its ways, but he knew the pain it could cause when used the wrong way. And I never saw that conflict more clearly than now. Part of him wanted to attack, but he didn't know whom to unleash his TempusCraft upon. Part of him wanted to throw his body in front of another to defend them, remnants of the Nomyd he would always be. But to protect whom? To attack one was to defend another. But who was right, and who was wrong?

We were all guilty of something, weren't we?

Everyone but me.

Ozmander's words came floating back to me, about me having a precious gift within me. Something so pure, even to name it was to jeopardize it.

And he knew that, how? I didn't even know!

He knew because he'd reached inside of me and touched my Sanctus and ripped the lid off of it. He'd established my connection to SanctusCraft and tried to teach me how to walk the straight and narrow path that it was.

And in doing so, he'd seen the depth of my innermost being.

"Rosalyn…" Ozmander took a step forward and I threw out my hand.

"Stop!" I shouted. "Stop, just everyone! Everyone…frr…"

There was a pain in my head, gnawing like a dog on a bone…grinding its teeth against my skull.

"Grraaah!"

Ilan rushed over to me and I pushed him back.

This wasn't happening…it wasn't…I didn't want it. *I DIDN'T WANT IT!*

Nurmedov grabbed Ozmander by the lapels of his tunic and lifted him up as he drove him back and smashed him into the nearest obelisk.

"What did you do to her? Huh?" Nurmedov shook him, his voice an animal growl through mashed teeth. "What the Hex did you do?"

Ozmander regarded him coolly and said only,

"It's what I *didn't* do that hurts her."

Nurmedov hauled back and smacked Ozmander with his fist and then let him fall in a lump as he rushed over to me. My head felt like it was going to explode. A million voices rushed through my ears on winds of stars and dust and broken memories.

Lives…lives…lives…all of them gobbled up and consumed…all of them stolen to feed the hunger of a man who'd lost his own…

I stood up on wobbly knees, finding Ozmander. A thin stream of blood trickled down the corner of his lip, making him look like the vampire that he was.

But I got it. I got it too well.

Ozmander had the ability to remove that block in people's Sanctuses. That was the rare and priceless gift *he* had. It was the beginning and the end of all the torment he caused. To reach into someone and flip the switch that made them who they were and protected that sacred substance from the rest of humanity.

All Sanctuses were blocked somehow. The stronger the Mystis, the stronger the block.

But as a man who could remove those caps and corks, those knots and locks, he had free reign to the Sanctus of every living thing.

And he ate them.

He ate them to gain power, build worlds, steal thoughts and ideas, savor emotions and memories not his own.

He was a thief of humanities, of life, of all that lived and moved and drew breath.

And he'd stolen every tangible and intangible thing that constituted the essence of existence.

Except for mine.

He'd had it in his grasp...he'd caressed it with his fingertips...savoring its flavor, its scent. Something so pure and innocent.

Why? Why hadn't he taken it? Why hadn't he seen the blank paper and burnt it to a crisp? Why was I so special? Why did I touch him so dearly that he could not steal my Sanctus like he'd stolen entire worlds?

I ran over to him and fell on my knees.

"Why?" Tears were in my eyes. "Why me?"

"Because," he said, trying to sit up. Why did he look so frail now? So weak and tired. "There was something about you that I'll never understand."

"Never?" I wiped my eyes. "Please, what are you talking about?"

"It was your desire, Rosalyn. Your desire to help me." I felt my lip twitch as sorrows rained down my cheeks. "You didn't know what it was like to be the most wretched evil ugly detested creature the Woven Worlds had ever known. You didn't know the eons of guilt that plagued me. You didn't know the holes I've ripped in the stars by devouring the lives I have." His hand reached out to touch my cheek, to stay my tears. His touch was as cold as ice. "Yet you reached out to me to heal me. To save me. You touched me, not giving a damn about who I was or what I'd done. It didn't matter who I was to you, or what I had been, as long as you could help me and heal me, that's all you cared about. And look at you now, all the way across The Sea of The Dead to the heart of the abyss. Just to save me. Just to heal me. Just to bring me back."

I stood up slowly and took a step away from him. I was loosing my breath, my sanity, my identity. I was swirling in the tidal force that sucked everything dry. I was being crushed...

No...I put my hands to my head. It was my Mystis...my Mystis screaming like a horde of city rats in a block fire. Millions of thoughts jumping around like the fleas on their backs...the disease of it all. The disease of the Mystis.

You can't! You can't! You can't! The voice of my Mystis shrieked as logic and reason burned within me. The hot flames of SanctusCraft coming alive ate them up. Still, as reason and logic torched and crackled, succumbing to the rising tide of SanctusCraft, their voices cried out.

Impossible! Impossible! Impossible!
What will be done cannot be undone!
You will be lost forever! LOST!!!

I looked at him, Ozmander, destroyer of worlds, devourer of souls. My eyes were red-rimmed and my heart throbbed with pain.

"Do it!" I shouted. Nurmedov reached out for me and I slapped him away. Ilan pulled Nurmedov back and pointed to the dread warrior Ozmander had named as his own son. He was down from the pyramid now, waiting. Waiting for what?

For me.

Because I was going up there. Straight up to the top of that damned thing.

"Do it!!!" I screamed.

Ozmander pressed himself up slowly and walked towards me. His eyes were darker than ever, darker than the darkness that cloaked the top of the pyramid from our eyes and I nearly crumbled to my knees before he even reached me.

But as soon as he did, his hand was on my forehead, and I closed my eyes and felt the crushing weight of every single life he'd ever stolen be fused with mine as my Sanctus left my Tempus and the skin and bones that I had been fell to the ground with a thud.

THIRTY-NINE

To be free of my Tempus was to break the surface of an endless ocean, gasp for breath, and stare at the sky, only to follow its curve to where sea met sky. Where infinity met infinity to the vanishing point. To be overwhelmed and lost in the magnitude of life, the gravity and scope of it. To see without detail, only excess. To be in my Tempus was to be bound to it, but to become nothing more than the essence of my personality and my innermost thoughts and feelings was to be free and eternal.

But if it felt like anything, I had become air and clouds, wind and stars.

Heavy air. Dark clouds. Fierce wind. Falling stars.

Because this wasn't the end of my life. It was only one moment of my journey. One moment so much greater than myself. One moment of cataclysm that demanded I deliver on my desire to help and heal. Not just Ozmander, but the millions of lives he'd ruined and stolen.

Because that's why I was here. To help and to heal. And without knowing it I would be able to undo a great and terrible travesty that had ripped a hole in the heavens.

It was the prophecy Ozmander had spoken to me, where I would be able to touch the past and the future at the same time and make a choice.

Forever.

Now where was I? Yes, standing right where I had fallen. Everything was the same, only strangely murky and distant, as if seen through a milky, silvery veil.

"Ilan, come here." Ozmander said, and something in his voice compelled Ilan to. "If you love her, guard her body with your life, do you hear me?" His hand went to Ilan's shoulder. "Do you hear me young man?"

He nodded quickly, paling at the thought of what that even meant.

"Guard her body with your life and kill anything or anyone that tries to take her."

Ilan flared his nostrils and nodded, unsheathing his rune sword and striding over to me. He was so brave, to be here, maybe not fully knowing why, other than for my sake.

If Ozmander was the reason I was here, *I* was the reason Ilan was here.

I wanted to reach out and touch him but I knew he wouldn't feel it.

"Thank you, Ilan." I told him, but his gaze was searching the dark dunes of dead sand and dust, spread out and around the temple. It was a massive waste of echoes and formless shadows. Hex knew what was out there.

But something was. Something hungry for my body. To steal it before I could get back into it. If that happened, well, then I would be forever detached from the realm of flesh and blood.

And in so much I had brought Ozmander back to this world the moment I met him on the road to Kalazaris.

Why? Why had I brought a mass murderer back to roam the earth?

Because he was a man, left for dead, frozen as he reached for the sun.

It didn't matter who he was. I'd taken an oath. And more than that, I was compelled.

In a world of death and decay, I had a commitment to life. To uphold it, to save it, to preserve it. To honor its sanctity.

"Nurmedov," Ozmander said, walking over to the adventurer who still held the opal knife at his side. "Nurmedov, listen to me. You can kill me when this is all over, but first you have to do this for me."

Nurmedov only looked at Ozmander, hollowed out and empty. His bravery was gone. So too, was his hatred. His eyes were the eyes of a little boy who had been left alone and abandoned. A boy who'd been spared when his own flesh and blood had died at his side, leaving him to roam the earth and figure out why.

Much like Ozmander's own son.

"Nurmedov, please. You have to do this. The fate of worlds rests on *all* of our shoulders. We *all* have to do our part. Especially you."

Nurmedov bit his lip and a single tear rolled down his left eye, as if the ice in them were melting.

"Wh…what is it?"

"I need you to swim across The Sea of the Dead and retrieve the dragons."

Nurmedov frowned.

"Is that it?"

Ozmander grimaced and nodded.

"That's it."

"Heh." Nurmedov scoffed. "I thought you were going to ask me to forgive you or something."

I wanted to tell him to be careful of Leviathan but Nurmedov was Nurmedov. He was afraid of nothing, save being alone again, of being that little boy.

Like the boy that hatred had raised. That boy that waited for us at the base of the pyramid. All grown up, pounded to brutal perfection on desolation's anvil.

Nurmedov ran over to Ilan and clasped him in a quick embrace.

"Take care of her." Was all he said, then he sprinted off into the darkness, his feet throwing puffs of sand and dust into the air.

Ozmander took me by the hand, and I could feel his touch as if we were two bodies, only his touch was no longer cold, but warm like a human hand. I didn't understand the transition of substance, but it was like he was more real to me than he'd ever been. More alive.

"Listen to me, Rosalyn," He said as we began to walk the obelisk-lined path, hand in hand. "This is not going to be easy."

"I know." I said.

"Look at the top of the pyramid."

Following his finger to the top of the structure, I saw what had been obscured in darkness when I had been bound to my Tempus.

A storm raged at the top of the pyramid. Furious clouds of violet and crimson swirled and warred, spitting bolts of ice blue.

This storm was bound to the peak of the pyramid, from which a thick, white hot rope of lightning sizzled and crackled. Raw and alive and hungry, it connected the pyramid, through this chain lighting, all throughout the abyss.

It was the nexus of his immortal power. The structure of his dark heart. The grave in which he kept all living souls to feed off their lives and thoughts and feelings and dreams.

"What do I do?" I said.

"You've got to get up there."

"That's it?"

"That's it. You'll know what to do when you're there. Trust me."

I did, as we walked forward. Free of my Mystis, trusting him was as easy as holding his hand.

And it was hand in hand we walked the obelisk-lined path to his son.

"Behold the Dark Lord Ozmander." The warrior said, his voice deep and rich and laced with sarcasm. "Forgive me if I don't bow."

Ozmander stopped. We were paces from the stairs. The purple and crimson storm above cast flashes of bruised light down upon us.

"Son, I'm sorry."

"It's too late for that."

"Would you believe that since that day your mother took you and your brother from me, that I have been looking for you?" I dropped my head to hear the throb in Ozmander's voice. It was an ancient pain I would never understand.

His son was unmoved. His heart was as hard and black as his armor.

"No."

"She hated herself for loving me. And I hated myself for loving her. But we both brought you and your brother into this world, and that meant we had the responsibility to raise you to something better than the war we were living."

And now it made sense. The vision I had when I touched the Pryystys of Thanem back in Kalazaris. The scene of two boys about to be sacrificed. The twin sons of Ozmander.

The boy's mother had been the High Pryystys of Thanem.

But that meant...

"Why did she want to kill you?" I asked.

The ferocious mask tilted my direction. I saw nothing in the void black eyes, but the voice rolling through the cruel smile of fangs chilled me.

"Who speaks?"

"Rosalyn De Boswel, a Nomyd."

"Do you like being out of your Tempus, Rosalyn?"

If it was meant to scare me, it worked. I threw my eyes back to Ilan.

Still vigilant, hard gaze set to the wild darkness, it was the stillness that shook me. The emptiness. The silence. Cold and cunning.

Something was coming for my body.

"What is your blasphemy?" The man said.

"Your mother." I said, taking a step forward. "She was going to sacrifice you and your brother on the altar of Thanem when you were only weeks old. A Paladyr rescued you."

The mask dropped and the man took a step forward. His voice, offhanded at first, gained spikes and thorns of bitterness.

"You speak the truth but you do not know the half of it."

"I say again, my son, I am..."

"I am *no* son of yours!" The man shouted, throwing an accusing finger in Ozmander's face. "I am my own man! When The Infernium learned of my parenthood, the Paladyr that saved my brother and I was sentenced to kill us both. The coward took us out in the wild and left us both for dead."

Ozmander sank to his knees.

"No..." He mumbled. "No..."

"That's right, *father*." The warrior sneered. "That gift of yours runs in the family."

My eyes fell to my feet. Anguish on Ozmander's behalf to realize what'd happened.

One brother had stolen the life of the other to survive.

Because their mother had stolen the children from their father.

Because their father had stolen the lives of entire worlds.

But the ground shook. Fists pierced the dusty gray sand all around the temple. Misshapen fingers of broken knuckles opened and flexed. Yellowed skin rose from the loose sand to reveal gangly arms and bony shoulders. Fat pink worms and white maggots wriggled along cavities and sores in the yellowy flesh, where skin and muscle had atrophied and decayed to reveal bleached bone.

"Do you know what that does to a man?" The warrior growled. "To devour his own flesh and blood to survive the wild? To swallow the soul of his own twin to see the sun for one more day?"

Ozmander could not speak. He could only weep.

The earth shook again.

Heads emerged from the sand, grotesque faces of half-eaten skin, rotting flesh hanging off their bleached skulls, mouths forever opened in a silent scream. Maggots dripped from the carved-out sockets of their eyes as their misshapen fingers dug for leverage in the loose gray sand.

Called to animation by the son of Ozmander, these disgusting and deformed undead pushed themselves from the sand, joints popping and snapping at the curses that gave them movement. From the whole crater of the temple they clawed their way up, lurching to height as gray dust emanated from them in eerie clouds. They stumbled forward, blindly, filled with the hatred of Ozmander's own son.

There were so many of them.

And they were all headed for my Tempus.

I turned back to Ozmander's son to see him throw his arms wide as two curved sabers of fire stretched forth from his hands. It didn't take The Learnyd to know what he was going to do with those sabers.

The low and rumbling voice of Ozmander's son shook the ground with unbroken fury. The flames of his sabers dripped and drooled fire and he flourished them over his head and leveled them at his waist.

"I AM NERGÜI, KING OF THE ABANDONED! HEAR MY RAGE AND KNOW MY PAIN!"

And then he charged us.

FORTY

Ozmander fell back from his kneel in a somersault and rose to a battle stance.

"Run!" He shouted, and swirled his hands to work a weapon as Nergüi unleashed his deathstrokes.

The fire sabers went *wumph* and *woosh* as they sought Ozmander's skin, and I sprinted to the side to hide behind one of the obelisks.

Throwing my glance back to Ilan, it was clear that he was in over his head.

The undead had arisen, possessed by Nergüi's lifetime of rabid anger and unfiltered rage and their deformed feet, dragging lines in the sand as they lurched and struggled toward him, would not stop until Nergüi's curse had been broken.

And how in the Hex were we going to do that?

I ran from the safety of the obelisk to the base of the pyramid and saw fire splash where saber met pike.

Ozmander had worked a pike of pure darkness, and it chilled me to know it'd been the very weapon he'd used in his wars against humankind.

His defense was clean and simple to stop Nergüi's storm of violence. It was like a tree against a hurricane. A rock buffeted by waves.

Waves of fire.

The pike in his gloved hands was a work of the black midnight sun, glowing with a dark and hungry aura. The black eye of death and gloom. Stretched out and sharpened to pierce the heart of any shield or plate.

Nergüi rattled his sabers to splash fire and hacked and slashed. Within the arcs of his sabers he threw out his foot to trip Ozmander or kick him square in the jaw.

Ozmander's pike soaked up each blow, and the flashes of fire cast eerie shadows on his face as battle transformed him. His eyes had grown darker still, as if all of his energy was in the pike itself. As if the blank space of true night was in his eyes, and his pike, and there was nothing between man and war. They were one and the same.

And all of his ability to suck the Sanctus from an entire world, to suck the will from his own son, had been focused to a single point.

Ozmander tumbled backwards as Nergüi pressed his assault once more. Dust coughed from the path between the obelisks and twin blades barely missed Ozmander's stomach, only to reverse and swing from opposite directions once more.

Nergüi was a beast, roaring as his arms wheeled and twisted like two independent limbs. Where one saber cut, the other sliced. Then both would crash down overhead and break off to launch themselves again at Ozmander and his dark pike, seeking any shred of unprotected space to slash and burn.

The dance of fire was hypnotic. Primal.

Back at my Tempus, Ilan prepared for war. He ached for it, bouncing on his toes, readying himself for the coming conflict. He knew that once it started, it would not stop till it was done.

Till nothing moved.

I watched as his eyes scanned each and every walking curse, back and forth, back and forth, as they ever so slowly closed in to surround him on all sides. To surround my Tempus. Their deformed limbs and grotesque expressions stretched out toward him, toward my flesh and bones, as if driven by insatiable hunger. By the purity of my body, the freshness of it. The heat. To touch it. To taste it. To rip it apart with their rotting nails and their broken teeth.

I was chilled again to think it, but it was true.

They were going to eat me.

And then Ilan.

But Ilan knew this was not a battle for TempusCraft alone. There were just too many of them. And so he did something that severed his tie to The Infernium once and for all and shocked me in the process.

He took the lion shield that Shmaila had give him and threw it on the ground. It landed with a dull thud and rattled around in the sand. Then he took something from around his throat...something attached to a very humble piece of string.

A vial.

Ilan opened the vial and poured it out upon the lion shield, upon the fierce face of hammered metal and jewels frozen mid roar, the eyes of rich garnet.

And then he bowed his head and said a few words.

By then the first of the undead was within his reach, and his rune sword flicked out to sever a limb. The undead didn't even notice. It kept coming, stretching for him with the other hand. Ilan chopped off that limb at the elbow and spun to remove the torso from the waist.

But then the hands he'd severed kept moving. They kept crawling for me. Digging through the sand. Stretching for me. For my hair.

Two more were upon him. Taller than him. Lumbering, staggering, getting in the way. Crowding him. Falling on him. Ilan cut them apart, deftly, but it wasn't enough. It would never be enough. They would keep coming, out of the ground, with their yellowy skin and mottled teeth, their empty sockets and silent screams. They would crawl and claw and bite and smother and suffocate till we had become just like them.

Bound, forever, to the abyss.

Ilan kicked one in the knee and split another in half before reaching down to grab my Tempus by the collar and drag me across the path, hacking and poking his rune sword into deformed limbs.

And that was when the lion arose.

Its roar was sharp and metallic, like the grinding of steel on a millstone. It emerged from the shield head first as if coming out of a barrel, or another plane of existence, its chiseled silvery body glistening wet with the liquid Ilan had poured on it. With its mane of emeralds and its claws of topaz, it leapt and tore at the undead with holy fury. The eyes of garnet seem to track a target even before the one it'd set itself upon had been torn apart, and with the lion, fearless and ferocious, I thought we stood a fighting chance.

That was until Nergüi knocked the pike from Ozmander's grip and kicked a cloud of sand and dust in his eyes.

Ozmander leapt backwards and fell, rolling and rising to meet the sabers of vengeance with his own bare hands. Reaching forth to meet the rage of his son. Swiping blindly at the air where his son had been.

A spiked gauntlet wrapped around his throat and fire ripped through his belly.

"Think that's the only thing I learned from you, old man?" Nergüi snarled. "You have no idea the things I know."

Nergüi twisted the saber and pulled it out. Fire licked through the hole in Ozmander's belly as if running along a fuse. Steam hissed and rose from his Tempus as fire melt ice.

And Nergüi's grip tightened.

Ozmander choked and blood drooled from his mouth, bubbling up his throat from the cauterized wound. He squeezed his eyes shut and gasped for breath.

But he was not dead yet.

Ozmander threw his elbows hard behind his waist to knock Nergüi back and turned to fight his son with whatever was left within him.

I had no words to wish him well.

All of my focus was on the steps before me and the swirling storm of crimson and purple at the top of the pyramid.

FORTY-ONE

The steps melted away, one by one. The sounds of battle faded in my ears.

Ghostly silence replaced the clashes and clangs, the tearing and ripping. The hurried mess of anything and everything, replaced with a resounding chorus of nothing. Not even the faintest whistle of the wind.

I felt so alone.

I looked up to the storm. It was the edge of another realm. Of something different. To ascend the pyramid was to transition between one and the other.

The further I climbed, the more I forgot about all that was beneath me. The more I detached myself from my Tempus and those fighting for it, the more I focused on what was before me, until I was running up the steps on my hands and feet, as fast as I could.

Closer to the storm. Closer to the colors till I was bathed in them. Closer to the bolts of energy shooting through it. Reaching out, reaching up. Running, stretching. Being lifted.

It was like feeling with senses I didn't even know I had.

And then I was in it. The storm. It was alive around me, a flurry of muted voices. Echoes of the unspoken. Bruised sounds. Muffled anguish.

I kept climbing.

I was possessed now. To reach the top. I had to. I *had* to. Bolts flashed past me in the swirl of color. Shocks of light snaking through the clouds. The clouds were rich with rage and I fought the urge to fall back into them. To be consumed in their power. To let the storm eat me. To be eaten.

Oh heavens, the undead had reached my Tempus. They were eating my Tempus.

Ilan...

The bolts zipped and flashed. They were hot, angry, cooking me as I climbed and climbed and climbed.

I couldn't think about it now. I couldn't think about anything but the top.

The top of the pyramid.

The top...

I stopped and looked down and wished I hadn't. Ozmander lay on the ground, sprawled out and exasperated. Nergüi stood over him. Proud. Hulking. Sabers low at his sides. Dripping flames. Was Ozmander dead? He looked dead. He wasn't moving. He was just laying there. Motionless. And Nergüi, King of The Abandoned. He just stood there, too. Staring at him. Staring at his father.

And then he turned to me. Slowly.

And pointed a saber at me.

I turned around and threw myself to the stairs and climbed. I climbed and climbed and knew he was coming for me. I could feel him. He was hunger. He was rage. He was the urge to kill. To devour. That brute. That black steel and spiked-gauntlet destroyer. He was going to catch me and hold me tight in a grip of thorns. He was going to squeeze and squeeze and squeeze. He was going to make me watch as the undead ate my Tempus bite after bite after bite. As they ate Ilan. Descending upon him like the maggots and worms in their own sorry skulls.

Oh Ilan...

I bit back the sorrow. I couldn't. I couldn't. I had to reach the top. I had to...

I had to...

Nergüi's spiked gauntlet wrapped around my ankle and I screamed. I looked down to see the creature of hatred and horror. The hulking monster. His cruel grin of fangs. His void black eyes. The swoop of his horns. The spread of his wings.

Nergüi's gauntlet constricted and the pain made me weep. I didn't have to understand it to feel it. I was no safer inside of my body than outside of it.

"Don't fight me." He growled. "Don't you dare."

Nothing but moans came from my mouth as I reached and stretched for another step. For another inch.

His grip slipped and I broke free for only the faintest moment as he attacked another step and caught my other ankle with his other hand. There was no escaping him. No matter how I struggled and stretched. No matter how hard I tried. There was no fighting this doom. This destiny. This death. This destruction.

But I kept stretching. I kept reaching. I couldn't stop. I didn't know how.

The hurt within me was that of a million souls. Of their cry to be restored to the world. Of their tears. Their blood. I wanted to help them. I wanted to heal their broken hearts. I wanted…

Nergüi's grip slacked and I gave the steps everything I had and then some. I didn't think about Nergüi anymore and pressed through the swirling storm of purple and crimson and stray bolts to reach the pinnacle of the pyramid where a large cauldron sat on a giant platform.

In the cauldron burned the life of every Sanctus Ozmander had stolen, hot and alive like the ever-changing eye of the sun.

It was life and lightning, searing and scorching and shooting straight up into the dark unknown of infinity above, and as I drew closer to the flaming cauldron of living lightning, I saw tiny filaments and strands, connected to it. Like ropes. I followed one out into the great depth of darkness above and squinted to see the faint twinkling of a star, and in that star an eye, and in that eye, a memory, and in that memory, a world that would never be forgotten.

Sorrow crushed me harder than the grip of the damned ever could. To think of all these lives, held captive. Of all these voices, silenced...of all these eyes and their brilliant beautiful colors. Shut, forever.

Overwhelmed, I staggered toward the cauldron. Oh, how it ached. How it ached for me to touch it. To touch it with the gift of healing that I had. To pour myself into it. To sacrifice my own existence for the healing of a million others.

Ozmander had said I would know what to do.

He was right.

There was nothing else *to* do.

In touching the cauldron, I would break the curse. I would release the locks and chains. I would sever Ozmander from his immortal power, from his knowledge of ages, from his wealth of humankind.

And I myself would cease to be.

That was the price to reverse Ozmander's curse. That was the secret.

It was because I was a Nomyd, and I had taken the oath. To save a life was to be bound to keep it.

So to end Ozmander's life would end my own. Because the only way I could break the curse was to take it myself. Within me, it would break into a million pieces, but in the process, so would I. That was the price of healing. That was the price of my touch.

And I did not care.

The voices of a stolen world would be no longer songless. The colors of eternity would be no longer bound within one man's bones. The lives of a million wayward souls would be no longer prisoner in ropes and chains, and the man named Ozmander would no longer roam the earth looking for redemption.

He would have it at last.

I closed my eyes and reached out to the flame. To the pure lightning of a million Sanctuses. Of memories and worlds.

And the fire burned me.

I opened my eyes with a hiss and found my hand at my feet.

Behind the wicked curve of his flaming saber, Nergüi's smile of fangs and derision mocked me for even trying.

For even hoping.

But he didn't know the half of it.

I reached down and picked up my hand and put it back on, healing myself in the blink of an eye.

"If that's all you can do, we're going to be here for a long time." He scoffed, scraping his flaming saber along the stone of the platform.

The sound of my own voice shocked myself. It was ferocious.

It was a roar.

I threw myself at him and pushed him off the top of the pyramid, locking arms with him and tumbling into nothing. Kicking and punching and screaming as we plummeted down down down to the gray sand below.

FORTY-TWO

Color splashed as we fell into the storm. Stray bolts tore through the swirl of crimson and purple. Blinding flashes of light scattered around the bound-up rage, the toil of emotion. I could feel it. So deep within. To fall into the storm was to fall into a well of voices and hear them all say the same thing in a different language. Nergüi strained to get to me and crush me just as the voices were crushing him.

The storm faded quickly as we fell. So fast, so fast the blackness of the void was eating my Sanctus. All the voices silenced. All the colors ripped away with the speed of our descent.

Nergüi lashed out at me with a saber of fire as we spun and tumbled only to scream out in pain.

There was an arrow in his arm.

Blood welled black in his armored hand as he cupped it to the fresh wound. He pulled at it and screamed again, falling faster than ever.

Down down down.

The arrow mocked him, jammed in a chink in his armor near the elbow, and his agony filled the dead and lifeless void beneath the storm.

I wondered where the arrow had come from and the shadowed shape of wings passed over me. I reached out and felt fur.

Soft, cozy, dragon fur.

Nurmedov stretched for me and grabbed, of all things, my hair. But there was no pain. His hand passed right through me and I kept on falling.

Dismay tinted his sick and sweat-glazed face and he wheeled Bailey around for another pass at trying to get me. His misunderstanding of Craft was stronger than ever, and he hated the fact that the ghostly form of Rosalyn De Boswel could not be saved by his hand. That she looked real but somehow wasn't as real as she looked. That form and substance were different for a Sanctus than for a Tempus. That there were things at work that he didn't understand. And that he was a man of no Craft. Stripped of it by The Dark Lord Ozmander in the Battle of The Abyss. The only man left alive, Ozmander had rendered him Craftless. Unable to work in his Mystis, Sanctus, or Tempus. Cut off forever of any connection to Craft whatsoever.

I felt sorry for him. I didn't want to know that about him, but I did, and it made it all the more amazing that he'd made it out of the abyss alive.

Nurmedov called out my name but I couldn't hear him.

Daisey was flying toward me in a lazy arc and I fell right on top of her.

Simple creature that she was, she kept on flying, looping a nice long circuit around the pyramid.

Nurmedov caught up to me. I didn't know whose eyes were wilder, Nurmedov's or that of his dragon Bailey. The frozen ice in Nurmedov's gaze was silvery with exertion and excitement. He looked like he'd stared down Leviathan and somehow managed to live.

Because he had.

I'm sure I'd hear the story later, so long as there was something for him to munch on while he told it.

"Where's Nilius?" I called out as our dragons flew wing to wing.

"He didn't make it." Nurmedov shook his head, looking down on the ravaged battlefield the temple had become. "What about…Ozmander?"

"I don't know."

I looked down, too. Ilan was beset on all sides by the undead. Relentless, they were possessed to rip him apart. Their twisted claws of hands scraped and snapped at his artistic form, ripping and tearing through hordes of them with his slender rune sword. The ferocious silver lion fought on tirelessly, but there were just too many. Their deformed faces howled their hunger and their hands, severed or not, kept stretching and reaching to pull Ilan down to the dust to die their horrible death of disease and decay.

"The kid's gonna die if we don't get down there." Nurmedov wheeled Bailey around and the dragon flapped his wings hard, shooting down the pyramid like an arrow. Daisey followed, just with little to no urgency, and I didn't know how to motivate her.

To her credit, she'd made it this far on her own terms. I had to be fine with that.

When we reached the base of the pyramid, Nurmedov leapt off Bailey's back, tucked, rolled, and took his bow from his back to pin an undead to an obelisk with a pinpoint shot.

"Thanks for showing up!" Ilan yelled as he hacked, his words ragged and wheezing in his throat. His TempusCraft was clean and sharp, but like the edge of his sword, battle had dulled it so deeply, that he nearly fell as dead the moment he knew we had come to relieve him.

"Wouldn't miss this for the world." Nurmedov said, pegging two undead together, head to head, so they ran into each other and fell down. Then he stowed his bow and hefted my Tempus over his shoulder. "Come on kid, let's go!"

Two undead smacked into Ilan, one clamping his rotting teeth on Ilan's forehead, the other wrapping deformed arms around his waist.

The former Paladyr bucked and spun out of their holds, thrashing with his sword and shield until they were nothing more than chunks of flesh and bone.

"Kurush!" He shouted. "To me!"

The metallic lion froze as the undead swarmed around it, nearly swallowing its beautiful shape in clouds of dead sand and dust.

Ilan tapped his shield with his sword, *clang clang*, and the lion looked at him. Ilan froze as the lion stared at him with eyes of red garnet and hunger, dipped his head and shook it.

"Kurush?"

Again, the lion shook his head, his mane of emeralds hard and undaunted.

Ilan swallowed, sniffed, and nodded to himself. He bowed tightly to the silver lion and it flashed off in the darkness to attack the congested hordes of the undead as they sprung from the never-ending dunes.

Ilan staggered toward me and fell to his knees. He was dead tired.

I reached out and hugged him something fierce and he stood up, hugging me back.

"Oh Rosy! You're back!" He hugged me so hard.

"Easy, Ilan!" I gasped, and he stopped himself, shaking his head just to look at me. Flesh and blood. Alive. Whole. Real.

Yes it was true, I was back in my Tempus. I was no longer the pale ghost he had seen running around before.

But going out of my Tempus had shown me what needed to be done.

What *I* needed to do.

"Ilan, you have to get Nergüi."

"What?"

"Don't ask questions, just get him and bring him here. We'll put him on Daisey's back and fly him to the top."

"Where is he?"

"Over by the last obelisk. Quick!"

He ran off and I helped Nurmedov hoist Ozmander up onto Bailey's back.

"He's still alive." Nurmedov snarled.

"But that's what you want, right?" I said as we secured him to the saddle. "So you can kill him?"

"Something tells me that's not going to happen." He eyed me deviously. "Something tells me a bleeding-heart *Nomyd* is in charge of this whole blasted thing. Like we're all just going to hold hands and sing a song and it'll all be okay."

I couldn't help it since he was so sour about it all and he was so right.

I kissed him on the cheek and said,

"Now who's the prophet?"

He blushed something terrible and looked hopelessly puzzled and I slapped Bailey on the side. Still thinking about what I'd said and done, Nurmedov wasn't paying attention and nearly fell out of the saddle as the dragon flapped its wings and scattered dust.

Just a few strides away, Ilan was tying Nergüi down in Daisey's saddle. The hulk tottered and swayed and moaned. He was out of it after that nasty fall, but he was still alive. I figured he had brain damage, but I was counting on that damage. On all that bitterness. That hatred. Those unholy bonds, so strong, binding him down to a life of isolation.

Ozmander, Dark Lord of the Abyss. Nergüi, King of The Abandoned.

Yes indeed I needed them both to heal the hole in the heavens, the wound in the stars.

Daisey staggered under our collective weight and couldn't make it up in the air.

"Forget it!" Ilan said as he hopped off and ran for the steps to the pyramid. "I'll take the long way!"

I threw out my hand to stop him but before I could, Daisey began to flap her wings and I lost Ilan Braun in a massive cloud of sand and dust.

FORTY-THREE

It was surreal to scale the pyramid again, the massive, ominous structure that it was. As Daisey flapped her wings to drift around and spiral up its height, it reminded me of the spiral stairs we walked to reach the gates of the abyss. It didn't seem like that long ago, really. So much had happened and I hadn't even stopped to sort it all out within. And so I took a moment to think about what I was about to do. About what was required of me.

One act to sever, one act to heal.

When the time comes, do not close your eyes, Ozmander had said to me as we stood on The Sea of The Dead. *All will be revealed and the choice will be yours and yours alone. You will touch the past and the future one in the same just as it will touch you and you will be forever changed.*

I stroked Daisey's soft fur as I thought about it. If even just to soothe myself. To slow my breathing. My blood simmered in my veins to grab ahold of the finality of it all. The gravity of it, the scope. The millions of lives entangled within the nexus of one single moment in space and time.

Would it be as easy to heal as it had been to hurt?

Higher and higher we soared, closer and closer to the irreversibly of it all.

Your choice will mark your days forever, and the days of those yet to come.

I saw Nurmedov out of the corner of my eye, rising up to sail right through the storm. To punch a hole in its scattered bolts and furious energy. His icy eyes were fierce. His face a shield. Nothing would stop him.

I marveled at him, at his bravery, and how it maybe even bordered on madness. How a man without Craft and the understanding thereof could sail straight into the eye of the storm and not even blink an eye.

Did he count the cost? Could he count it all as loss if I failed to do my part? What was left for him, when revenge had been taken from him?

What remained?

And then I spied the silvery form of Ilan, running up the pyramid steps like a blur of silver. A smeared streak of mercury.

It hit me, stuck in the flesh and bone of my Tempus. The bravery of these two men. The heroic feats they could achieve through the sheer power of their wills. Through the perfect symmetry of determination and desire.

Well, now *my* time had come to do the same.

Flying through the storm, I could see that Nurmedov reached the top before me and was already on his feet, untying Ozmander from the saddle. I threw a glance to Nergüi behind me, stretched across Daisey's back like an oversized rug. Even lying there, nearly lifeless, he was still so intimidating, so dreadful. I half expected him to roar to life and strangle me with one of his spiked gauntlets.

But he didn't. We reached the top easily and Nurmedov helped me secure Nergüi. When he couldn't untie the knots that Ilan had tied, he took one of his daggers and sliced the man free.

He fell with a *clank* on the top of the pyramid and rolled around, unconscious. I sighed and pressed my hands to my head.

"How can I help?" Nurmedov said, sheathing his dagger. When I just stood and stared and processed how it was all going to happen, he let his eyes wander up the bristling column of lightning shooting straight out the peak of the pyramid. He kept following it till he could lift his head no more and began to gaze around at the millions of tiny webs and veins of light stretched throughout the ceiling of the dome. Were there millions? Or tens of millions?

Even hundreds?

"Wish you'd stayed in Kalazaris?" I mumbled, rubbing my temples.

He shook his head, still captivated by the sight.

"A wise man once said that life is an adventure. To say no it is to let yourself die."

"Really?"

"No, I just made that up. Does it sound wise?"

Before I could say whether it did or didn't, Ilan rushed up the stairs and collapsed at Nurmedov's feet, his chest heaving as if his breath had run away from him and he had chased it down and tackled it, forcing it back in his lungs.

"You alright?" Nurmedov laughed. "I know you don't like flying but you can't run everywhere, you know. Your knees'll wear out by the time you're my age."

Ilan groaned to push himself up.

"Aren't you like...thirty?"

"No, I'm ageless."

"You *are* not."

"You're right, I'm twenty eight and thirteen twelfths."

Ilan frowned.

"Wouldn't make you twenty-nine?"

"Guys!" I shouted, throwing my hands out. "I have to think!"

Both of them looked at me, chastised for a moment. But I realized, no, I *didn't* have to think.

That was just my Mystis, the strongest and most developed muscle within me, wrestling with what I knew I had to do. With what was so easy to do when I was simply my Sanctus, free from flesh and bone.

What I had almost done myself, before Nergüi had sliced my hand free from my arm.

Touch it. Touch the lightning.

"Oh boy..." I said to myself. "Here goes nothing."

I moved closer to the living rope of energy.

"Nurmedov!" I shouted. "Get Ozmander and hold him on my right side. Ilan, get Nergüi and hold him on my left. If they're wearing gloves or gauntlets, take them off."

They complied as quickly as they could, but the raw torrent of energy spooked them. Its voice was a hoarse whisper, a sucking funnel of worlds colliding and human lives ebbing and flowing like tide. They stared at me with wide eyes as I drew closer. And closer.

And closer.

"Here you go." Ilan said, and stood Nergüi up on his feet. He was so tall. He swayed and threatened to keel over but I grabbed his hand and held on tight. Unlike his father, his hand was searing to the touch, and as I held on I began to sweat.

"Come on...come on..." Nurmedov said to Ozmander, who was in worse shape. My eyes fell to the wound in his belly, ugly and black where Nergüi's saber of fire had cut and cauterized one and the same. His face was paler than when I had first touched him on the road to Kalazaris, when our fates had first intertwined and tangled themselves together. Nurmedov inched him closer and closer and finally I grasped his hand and held on tight.

It was colder than ever. I ground my teeth together at the antagonism. At the conflict. My Tempus felt it as their auras and emotions leaked into me. Splitting me in half with ice and fire.

Nurmedov and Ilan were about to back away.

"Move them closer." I shouted, my forehead glazed with sweat as my body began to shudder with chills. They looked at each other, hesitated, and then followed orders.

Closer we all came to the lighting, closer to the blazing root of a million of lives.

I couldn't see through it, but I knew they were close enough. Close enough to make this work. I squeezed their hands tight and bowed my head.

And closed my eyes.

FORTY-FOUR

Everything changed in one breath, when Nergüi reached out and took his father by the hand. Holding tight and squeezing as if to rid a sponge of its liquid, I felt the cavernous roar of hunger within him. The aching need for the one that created him.

I tasted the raw sorrow of being abandoned. Forced to survive in the wilds by stealing the life of his own twin brother, who by chance had been weaker than him. Something he inherited from the one who created him. From the Dark Lord Ozmander.

And the regret, the damnation of his actions falling upon us all like rain.

Possessed by my desire to heal the broken and help the wounded, I pulled us all, hand in hand, into the bristling cord of lightning.

Countless memories flooded me in waves. Echoes of humanity, glittering like stars. Languages I did not know, rising and falling with every color of the sun. Time stretched out, uncoiled and decompressed, and we stood there, connected together in the nexus of worlds and a Sanctus lost.

"Nergüi!" I shouted through the sucking wind of the nexus, screaming over the wild power of the millions of lives Ozmander had bottled up and bound within the pyramid. "Nergüi!"

I heard only a moan as he released his sorrows. Choking. Bitterness and rage falling free from whatever color eyes sat beneath that fearsome mask.

"Rosalyn!" The voice of Ilan lashed out to me. So distant, as if beneath the waves of the sea. "Rosalyn they're coming!"

Who? Who was coming?

"The undead, they're scaling the pyramid! And they're not using the stairs."

Oh great...

"Nergüi, listen to me," I shook his hand and squeezed it. "You wandered because you had no home. You named yourself because you had no name. You killed because you had no choice."

Again he moaned, his whole body heaving as the energy of millions swirled around us.

"But that's who you were. Not who you can be. Not who you want to be."

"I am what I am." He sobbed. "I am what I have been made to be. Twice the son of hell that my old man was."

"No!" I shook his hand. "No! That's not true! You can be free of your past! You can be free of the guilt, you can leave it all behind and walk the other way!"

Nergüi shook his head as the conflict forced him to his knees. To go with him, I broke contact with Ozmander and joined both my hands to Nergüi. I crawled to him and threw my arms around him and hugged him. He squeezed me so tight I thought I was going to suffocate, and he cried so hard I thought he was going to drown us all. His armor was wet with sadness.

"Leave it, Nergüi. Leave who you were behind in this place. Let it all die. Let your hatred die with your memories. Let your grief die with your regret. Let Nergüi die and walk away from him."

I stretched to reach up and remove the fearsome helmet of wings and horns and cruelty. Slowly, it came off, and he didn't stop me. He only cried and cried and once the helmet was off I threw it as far as I could.

"Rosalyn!" A voice called from outside the cord of lightning.

"Not now!" I called back.

"Rosalyn! The undead are gone!"

"Good!"

"But it's...it's...Rosalyn get out of there now!" There was so much desperation, so much I didn't know if the voice was from Ilan or Nurmedov.

I ignored it and took Nergüi's face in my hands.

"Look at me." I said. He wouldn't, his head bowed in shame, his memories still too raw. "Look at me." I said again, and bent lower to meet his eyes with mine.

They were brown, like dirt. Not black, like his father's. Brown. Warm like a dark floor in a room with a fire when the world blew cold and wild outside. Brown eyes in a slender face with a weak jaw and a heavy brow. Sunken so far into the skull it was like they wanted to disappear.

"Whoever you are," I said, "You're not the man you used to be. Forgive your father and your mother and forgive *yourself*. Be Nergüi, King of The Abandoned no more. Rise up and be a new man, not the son of your old man. Rise up to never again know the hurts and hatreds of the one you were, but begin to know the healing of a new man."

And when he looked at me, he looked me in the eyes, and felt the connection of the nexus around us coming into focus. As if every voice swirling around in every language was pulling for the same thing, yearning for the same thing. For me to touch his forehead. For me to break the power of the curses. For me to take the keys and the locks that'd bound up an entire world under Ozmander's control and destroy them with the very same power that'd been bound up.

But that meant...

Ozmander.

I stood up and looked around frantically. It was impossible to see through crackling current of lightning and the torrent of voices. Especially as they kept screaming at me to reach out and touch Nergüi. To connect in order to sever.

But Ozmander, that meant he would die?

How was I supposed to bring him back if he was going to die?

"Rosalyn!" Someone screamed from just behind me and I knew that it'd all come to a point. A point beyond the irreversible. All would be changed by my choice, and I knew the right one. I had already made it within. The one I would make a million times over again because I had a million reasons to do so.

I ran to Nergüi and laid my hand on his forehead. The weight of a forgotten world crashed at my back like a wave of water as tall as the pyramid itself. Above us, the star of every stolen Sanctus fell with a symphony of streaks. Tears of light. The man known as Nergüi sucked in a breath of air, as if breathing for the first time. The weight of the world Ozmander had consumed crashed upon us and we felt it rush and break apart and every Sanctus fly away, back to the world that had been theirs just as this one was ours.

And for the first time, I tasted healing, sweet like fresh honey on my tongue.

For my whole life, I had only known the taste of its need, and how nothing I could ever do was good enough. Ilan had been driven to The Infernium by that need, and I had been driven to the top of the class to be the best Nomyd student Bayh had ever seen. Only to set out for Kalazaris and find I didn't know the first thing about healing now that I'd actually healed someone and knew what it was to do so.

It had nothing to do with all the information I had collected, or all the tests I had taken. It had to do with compassion. Mercy. Grace. Humility.

And love.

It was about touching someone's Sanctus with your own and lifting them up. Holding on to them and never letting them go.

Because I knew, down to the depth of my being, what it felt like to turn a lost key in an indestructible lock and shut the door to one world by opening the door to another. I knew what it meant to silence an eternal echo by creating a louder one that rang out in opposition.

I knew what it meant to take the darkness and drive it out with the light.

With the freedom of forgiveness.

It meant to make a connection that could not be broken, and to fight for that person on the other side of the rope.

And if that was the end of it, I would've been so very happy.

But it was not.

FORTY-FIVE

The blinding cord of bristling lightning had fizzled away, leaving the death and decay of the abyss to fill my sight.

The parched dunes and scattered ruins of the temple, the barren void above.

And the gigantic mass of serpentine flesh, slithering through the darkness.

I moved to react, to do something. To do what? I don't know, something, but before I could, Leviathan released his roar and turned all my bones to liquid.

Only Ozmander reacted, rising from the heap he had fallen to, his eyes alive and unblinking in his skull.

"Ozmander!" I shouted, but he could not hear. There was a call more powerful than mine pulling at him.

I stood my ground in the middle of the pyramid's peak as Ozmander walked to the edge. The others gathered behind me. For some reason, at a time when fear needed to be the furthest thing from us, it had gathered them all together at my back. Maybe it was awe. Maybe it was just being so overwhelmed by the ancient evil that was sliding and snaking through the darkness.

But Ozmander had been so moved to rise from the door of death and stride to the edge of the pyramid. To be seen. To be filled. And as he did so, two dots of white hot energy pierced the murk.

And grew. And grew.

And grew.

The dots were eyes, impossible to look away from. Two white orbs of fallen stars deep set in the massive mountain of a long and ugly snout. Hungry and greedy, the eyes were set aflame by the man that had responded to the roar, and the mouth of the beast opened wide to reveal rows and rows of curved teeth, lined within its stone-like jaw as if they were the battle lines of armies waiting for war.

The beast stared at Ozmander and watched as the man stretched his hands out and closed his eyes, and the beast began to breath deeper and deeper, working itself into a frenzy, its eyes swelling with malevolence.

And the beast heaved from deep within the length of its armored belly, shaking and twisting and wriggling to spew a river of purple flames.

I covered my face by instinct but Leviathan was upon us, pouring purple flames all around the pyramid, soaking the sunken realm of the temple in a lake of fire. The fire spread and spread, till there were no more dunes to see. No more temple relics, no more ruins.

Just flames, as purple as a bruise.

Still Leviathan spit flames from the bottom of his belly, roaring and shaking and slithering into the choked mess of purple fire.

Heated just to his liking.

And the beast, seemingly never ending as he slithered and swam in the flames, wrapped the steely sinews of his massive body around the pyramid and brought his enormous face to see the man named Ozmander eye to eye.

"My Gyyd..." Ozmander intoned. "Am I not powerful in your sight?"

It was a voice of stone grinding against stone that responded. Cruel with ambition. The twisted thinking of vanity glazed Leviathan's gaze as he beheld Ozmander, the beast he had created.

"My son, you are the most powerful man that has ever lived. Inhale the scent of my fires, let them feed your lust for another world. Bring me more souls my son, I am so very hungry."

Ozmander inhaled and tipped his head back blissfully.

And I was gutted.

My jaw was slack, I could not believe what I was seeing or how it made me feel. I just...I couldn't. I felt so betrayed, hurt, wounded, destroyed.

But there was the sound of something being torn behind me and I glanced.

It was a spiral, like something telescopic stretching out and piercing one plane with another. I frowned as what looked like a fist ripped and punched through the space just behind Ilan.

The hole stretched and stretched and shredded.

And Shmaila jumped out.

Everyone reacted with varying degrees of surprise but none of us moved. Shmaila's face was set for war and she rushed to me, her dreadlocks bouncing as she did.

"Everyone get inside the tunnel! Everyone!" She pointed to the hole she had made. "Run!"

She came to me, and her touch was cool and refreshing, comforting me, telling me how feverish and sick I felt without actually knowing it.

"That means you too, Rosalyn."

But I couldn't move.

"But I need to bring him back!" I said, exasperated, looking past the man who I knew I never should've trusted but did. The man who I knew had helped me *somehow*, he had taught me *something*, right? I couldn't just leave him here.

Didn't I owe him as much? As much to at least...*try*?

"Rosalyn, leave him."

"No!"

"Rosalyn, he is given himself over to Leviathan! Can't you see?"

Yeah, I could see. I saw it and it scared the snot out of me. I felt the power he was getting, stoked like the bellows of a smithy, fed and fed and fed with the greed that could eat an entire world and everything inside of it. Forged into a weapon of mass destruction.

I could feel it cooking his Mystis inside of his skull. *My son, you are the most powerful man that has ever lived. Bring me more souls my son, I am so very hungry.*

But I could touch him, and bring him back. Turn him away from it all. Couldn't I?

I took a step forward. Shmaila grabbed my arm.

"No Rosalyn. To even try it is to embrace the very thing you want to save him from."

I looked back at him, at Ozmander, and beyond him, at the massive snout of Leviathan, the rows and rows of his curved teeth. Shmaila shook my arm again.

"No Rosalyn. You're playing with fire."

I looked behind me. Ilan and Nurmedov were helping Nergüi get into the hole. He was staggering and numb, stripped of all the hatred that'd made him so powerful. A hollow shell of what he'd made himself to be. A shadow. A shadow disappearing into Shmaila's tunnel back to safety, away from this mess, where he could be nurtured. Where the change within could take roots in good soil. Nurmedov was even calling to the dragons and they were flying into the hole, too. The tunnel, she had called it. The way out.

The way out of all of this mess, this craziness.

But to leave would be to turn my back on him. On Ozmander.

To turn my back on the Nomyd code.

"Rosalyn…"

"What about Nergüi?" I said. "He was worse than his father, wasn't he?"

"He was but don't you know how badly he wanted to change?"

"And Ozmander?"

"He fed you lies, Rosalyn, just as he fed me lies. Just as he fed himself lies. Every lie is founded in a grain of truth. Whatever he told you or me or anybody was just true enough to get us all to go along with it. To be here. Leviathan had corrupted his Mystis with his twisted poison so badly he could no longer think any other way. He was so deceived, so very deep down within, to believe that he could return to the home of his power and turn his back on it."

Leviathan roared once more and Ozmander turned to face us.

"Rosalyn…" He said, and my blood ran cold. It froze me to hear his voice and the pain within. Surely, wasn't Ozmander a prisoner in his own skin? Couldn't he be saved from the curse of who he was?

"Rosalyn don't go. Don't leave me down here."

My face twisted with emotion. Torn.

"Rosalyn, don't listen." Shmaila begged me, and let go of my arm. She would not force me.

She would trust me.

"Rosalyn, you know me." Ozmander said as Leviathan rose higher and higher behind him, his breathing slowly increasing, breath by breath, as fire stoked within. "Rosalyn I reached deep within you…I could've stolen your life. But I didn't…why would I do that if I was such a bad person?"

"Grrnnn…" I smashed my palms into my eyes. I couldn't do it. I couldn't leave him.

And I couldn't stay here.

I couldn't…

I…

"Rosalyn, look at me." Ozmander took a step toward me and stretched out his hands.

I opened my eyes to see fire consuming his hands, purple and cold and dripping on the stone below.

His eyes were glazed with the cast of the purple flames, and his black armor gleamed like a dark jewel. His cape of ermine was soaked in purple fire and he stepped closer and closer, his arms wider and wider, as Leviathan rose higher and higher.

I looked at Shmaila.

"He's right, he didn't steal my life when he could've. Why not?"

Shmaila didn't answer.

Ilan did.

"That's because he wanted me."

I spun around, expecting Ilan to be long gone. But there he stood, looking like a sculpture poured of liquid silver. His rune sword was low in his grip and his silver shield that'd once displayed the lion Kurush was just an empty circle.

"What?"

"If he could corrupt you then he could corrupt me, if he could corrupt me, he could corrupt the Shukach, and there would be no one to stop him from going world to world, eating everything in his path."

Shmaila stood defiantly at his side, supporting his words, and still Ozmander advanced. His words were razor sharp.

"True as that may be, what are you going to do about it?"

I turned back to Ozmander with a sigh and wiped a tear from my eye.

"I'm going to thank you for all you've taught me and say goodbye."

The reality was slow to sink in.

"What? You're not going to fight me?" He roared. "I will rise from this pit and consume all that you hold dear!"

"No you won't." I said, turning my back on the man I never knew and joined Shmaila and Ilan in the tunnel Shmaila had Crafted as Leviathan greedily eyed the man before him and could stay his hunger no more, falling upon the Dark Lord Ozmander with row upon row of wicked curved teeth.

And as the hole sealed up behind us, I wondered if I heard laughter, or weeping, or a raging torrent of flames burying the ancient pyramid in a blaze of darkness, or if I heard anything at all.

Anything but my own heart beating slower and slower in my chest as Shmaila reached out and grabbed my hand and held it tight.

FORTY-SIX

We walked and walked and Shmaila held my hand until we reached the surface. With every steep step up the shaft she had Crafted to fold the distance between the peaceful surface of the island and the awful abyss, darkness ebbed away and light returned. The crushing burden of the great beneath was replaced, moment by moment, by the easy sea breeze and the woosh of the wind. It was like catching my breath after a flat out sprint, or becoming whole once again after a terrible sickness.

Or waking up from the worst of nightmares.

Every step drove me further and further from the horrors of the abyss, and pushed me closer to the sun and the promise of a new day and a new season in my life. Strangely, I felt like I was finally about to walk in what I had always wanted to but never knew how.

I just never thought it'd happen like this.

I shed tears to remember Ozmander and just wordlessly shook my head at it all. At the gravity of it. Shmaila squeezed my hand to let me know it would be okay. That some things in life just wouldn't make sense to me until I'd lived through them and learned to sort them out in retrospect. And I knew the more I walked away from it all the more perspective I would gain.

Even when there was still something throbbing inside of me, an emptiness that couldn't be filled.

At least not yet.

And when Shmaila's tunnel finally ended and we crawled up on to the solid ground of beach grass and freedom, the sun greeted us with its perfect light and heat, high above, juicy and orange. Nurmedov fell to his knees and sighed, staring at it in awe.

"How I have missed you." He said to himself.

"I could say the same of you." Ilan whispered to me.

Bailey took off running and kicked around the wispy white grass, running and running and running as the sea wind so inspired him. Occasionally he would dig his wet black nose into the ground and paw at something, only to raise it to the wind once again and fly off in another direction. Occasionally his wings flapped and he seemed to skip across the rolling hills, loving life.

Daisey trotted off to find herself a relatively flat space of earth and plopped down for a long nap, eventually rolling onto her back and letting her ears flop wide on the ground. I could even see her missing teeth, just like it had been the first time I'd ever seen her in Kalazaris. Perhaps heaven was just a place where she could close her eyes and feel the sun shine on her belly.

I looked around for Nergüi but could not find him.

"He is not far." Shmaila said, rubbing the small of her back as she peered over the rolling hills of white grass. "He needs a few moments alone, I would think."

I nodded, and Shmaila let her gaze drift between me and Ilan, and then a little smile wriggled across her lips and she said, "I will see if Nurmedov is hungry."

I peeled off my helmet and gave the sun a glance. It was so beautiful, so real and alive, yet so very distant. How I had taken it for granted. How I had taken the beauty of Bayh for granted. The trickling creek and the whispering trees. The tall stone walls and the comfort of dusty books. Only to realize there was an ugly world out there. Worlds without hope, without a voice, without anything to hold near and dear except pain and anguish, sorrow and suffering.

Worlds of dirt, death and darkness. Bones and blood and broken things. Bleak and black and broken by those born of the abyss.

How I craved to change that.

One life at a time.

I reached for the clasp to my cape and Ilan stopped me.

"Let me help you with that."

I smiled and said,

"It's not *that* heavy."

"I know." He took it and folded it carefully, his blue eyes seeming to study every flake of dust and smear of dirt. Remnants of the near past. Remnants of something the bright and beautiful sun was pushing into a memory, dimming with every breath.

"I...I don't know what to say." He mumbled, his lips flat. He shrugged. "Now that it's over and you actually *can* go back to Bayh with me...I can't ask you to."

"Because *you're* not going back?"

He nodded. His jaw looked even stronger than that first day I'd seen him in Kalazaris. His eyes glossy with a deeper current.

"I can't. I can't touch something greater than myself and shrivel away into the shadows. I'd be so convicted. I wouldn't be able to stand the sight of my own face in the creek."

"You can take a moment to think about it."

"No." He shook his head, and handed me back my cape. "I know my place. I always did. I just never knew how to get there."

Then Ilan looked me square in the eyes.

"It took me running away from you to realize just how much I love you, Rosalyn. But it took being with you once again to realize just how different we are."

I let his words run through me with the heat of the sun. I knew what he meant. What he was saying.

"I know, Ilan. I feel the same way. I can't even describe what I felt when I saw you again. You were my dearest friend in the whole wide world and then you ran away. You abandoned me. Even though there was nothing else for you to do, I still felt so horrible that last year, when studies were the hardest. I guess I knew in the smallest way how Nergüi felt, to survive by himself. I think if you'd been there with me I would've been so happy just to graduate. But without you I was driven to the top of the class. In spite of you or something. Lot of good it did me." I shrugged off the memory. "But to see you again, in the square...and to see how different you were...it's like you finally looked the way you felt that last year before you ran away. Like the outside of you finally matched up with the inside."

"Really? You saw it coming?"

"Yes...with all the time we spent together, I knew we were growing apart in so many ways and growing closer in every other."

"I think that's what I'm saying." His head drooped, as if it weighed a thousand pounds. "I love you now more than I ever have." There was a throb in his voice and he cleared his throat. "And I think that's because I have to say goodbye to you again."

I took his hands in mine. They were so much bigger. And stronger. Roughened by the hard work it'd taken for him to make Paladyr at such a young age.

"But you're not running away this time, Ilan. You're walking toward that which you believe gives you purpose. What you can do that no one else can. That's amazing." I squeezed his hands and smiled and let my joy seep into him. "Just think how many crusty old men used to ask the new year's class, so what do you want to be when you grow up? You always knew but you didn't feel you could say it. Like they'd shoot you down and say you *couldn't* do what you knew down in your bones you *had* to. *They* pushed you away to something that wasn't true to you but *now* you can go get it. Now you can be what you know in your heart you always wanted."

"Even if I didn't know what that was?" He half smiled. "I'd never even *heard* of the Shukach."

"Well, I'm sure they've heard of you. They're probably getting ready for you now."

"Still...I mean...I have to travel halfway across the world just to get there. It's like this secret place in the mountains. I don't know the language. It could take me a year to get there, and then they could reject me, or I could crap out in training."

"Oh Ilan." I touched my hand to his forehead. "Put that Mystis to rest and put one foot in front of the other. And before you know it, I'm sure our paths will cross again."

Ilan smiled and then hugged me tight. A bit too tight. Actually, he crushed me. I felt his love as still my dearest friend in the world but it was impossible to breathe. Perhaps he forgot about his armor. That and his being gifted with TempusCraft and having physical strength that I couldn't even fathom.

I heard someone clearing their throat behind him and he backed away politely. It was Nurmedov, holding a half-eaten drumstick of some sort of fowl. Spiced and roasted, by the look of it.

"Hey, as long as you're giving out hugs!" Nurmedov moved forward to Ilan and when Ilan frowned at the absurdity of hugging a man, Nurmedov laughed, punching him in the shoulder, saying, "Relax brickface."

He turned to me, his icy eyes as bright as a winter sky and full of the same brisk joy.

"So Rosalyn," He took a bite of fowl and spoke with his mouth full. "Since I'm going to escort this big lug all the way to the home of the Shukach, what are your plans?"

My eyes wandered over to Shmaila who smiled warmly.

"I have a lot to learn."

"You?" Nurmedov scoffed. "Thought you were a Nomyd."

I couldn't help but laugh. It sounded so weak in retrospect. Something I had prided myself on, just as Ozmander had prided himself on all the things he had done. In the end, no matter what the scale, pride was pride, and to be the healer I wanted to be I would embracing the very opposite virtue.

Humility.

To see no moment as insignificant, and no human life as worth less than mine. To see every moment with the hope of redemption and look every pair of eyes I crossed paths with *in the eyes* so that they knew I would lay my life down for that Sanctus even if they spit in my face and walked the other way.

To heal was to touch a Sanctus with your own and share the pain, to get your hands dirty in the filth of another and tell them you would never leave them or turn your back on them. You would be right there with them, through every fractured moment, till the breaks and tears had been mended and restored.

As long as it took.

And I knew that the more I could submit to Shmaila's wisdom, the more I could help people.

Starting with Nergüi.

And it's not like Shmaila was a dry and dusty old man behind an ancient desk. Every time she held my hand I felt peace resonate within me and every time she looked me in the eyes I knew the answer to a secret riddle was just one word away.

In this I felt hope, just as salty and fresh and raw as the sea and sunlight around us, and I knew that day by day by day, it would all be okay.

So long as I never forgot what it was that made me who I am. Why I am. What I am.

Rosalyn De Boswel, healer of the broken.

EPILOGUE

The cold wind knifing across the scrubland steppes was a cruel master, slashing at anything and everything between the Eastern Spine and the trade roads of the Sun's Edge, and had been driving the two men further and further from civilization for nearly a month. The mirth of traveling markets and minstrels long deaf in their ears, only the wind and the plod of footsteps remained, digging through the silence one moment at a time. Before them, jagged mountains of blue diamonds punched through cloaks of snow and ice like teeth and steel caught in eternal struggle. Ancient, indomitable, and defiant, the peaks were home to the Shukach and all of their secrets.

The shorter man threw a sour look to the distant peaks. They were mirrors of his eyes. Sharp, cold, and forged by the anvils of time. The wind howled again as he took a final bite of an apple nearly the same color as his lips.

"Bah." He threw it to the ground, causing it to roll and skip across the scruffy grass. "Pithy crap. Waste of coin."

"Relax." The taller man said. Though he was younger than the shorter man, the journey had aged him greatly. His blue eyes were weathered and guarded, his posture artistic and lean. Remnants of his youth had all been eroded away by the path he had chosen. "You'll be home soon enough."

Still hungry and unsatisfied, the shorter man watched the half-eaten apple roll to a stop and chewed on his lip. The faint reminder of a road split before them, veering off in two very different directions. One led north, parallel to mountains lost and forgotten by the maps of man. The other road led straight into the scrubland and steppes, were it grew dizzy and treacherous and disappeared. The shorter man with four daggers strapped to his chest and a honeywood bow at his back placed his hands on his hips and squinted out into the horizon where the sun had not yet risen, but stretched a band of violet along the curve of the earth. Past where the fertile valley of his ancestors welcomed the light of the newborn sun in every stalk of grain and every leafy tree, to where his beloved Matriarch Khurshid the Great waited to see him once again, the prodigal son of many wars.

"You are right, my friend." The shorter man said and turned to his companion. "And this is where I leave you."

He reached out his hand and the two embraced with one hand clasping the other, the other hand touching the shoulder of the other.

"With everything you ever learned, I'm sure." The young man laughed.

"Not everything." The man named Nurmedov winked. "None of my bad habits, for sure. And nothing I know about women."

The former Paladyr named Ilan Braun laughed. It was the sound of water trickling through a brook. A laugh of reminiscence. A virtue closely guarded behind eyes that missed nothing.

"You taught me nothing about them because you *know* nothing about them."

"Not true." Nurmedov scratched a beard grown thick by the journey. "I know how much they love me."

"Yeah, so much so no woman has spoken to you since we left Perisaris. And *that* was because she remembered you from a time she saw you in Kalazaris, if I recall."

"Enh." Nurmedov shrugged. "Makes sense, right? They all avoid me because they like me so much?"

"Right." Ilan smiled and turned his gaze to the shorn peaks. "I'm sure if there are any women up in those mountains, any women in the Shukach, and they give me a reception as cold as this wind is, I'll just remember the wise words of a bearded man. It's because they love me."

Nurmedov shrugged again, but this time with a cheeky smile.

"Let it never be said I didn't teach you everything I know."

Again the men embraced, and Ilan said, "Thanks for nothing," and smiled as Nurmedov hitched his pack on his shoulders and strode off into the rising sun.

A few paces from Ilan he called back.

"I really should go all the way with you. You know, see that you make it safely there and all."

"You're not my mother." Ilan shouted into the wind.

"Yeah..." Nurmedov grew smaller and smaller as he walked and the scrubland swelled around him. "I just hate to think of you climbing those mountains alone, you know?"

But the smile on Nurmedov's face was keen as he finally turned around and set off to the valley of his ancestors for good.

Nurmedov knew there were some things a man had to do by himself. Sometimes those were what made a man the man he was, and they had to be done alone.

"Thanks for nothing, Nurmedov." Ilan sighed ruefully as he lost his companion in distance and wind. "But I'm not alone."

He looked around as the wind howled something fierce. All the grass whistled and shook and the loneliness sank in.

Ilan removed the shield from his back. It was flat and round and looked like a silver serving tray that had since lost its polish.

A smile slowly stretched across Ilan's face and he drew his slender rune sword from its sheath. Steel was a quiet whisper against the raging wind.

Clang clang. Ilan hit the shield with his sword and waited. When nothing happened, he peered across the scrub and *clang clang clang* hit the shield again.

Sure enough, padding up through the lumpy terrain was the form of a lion, a lion made of silver and precious stones, and a heart that would never die.

"Kurush." Ilan kneeled as the lion came up to him. "Kurush, I knew you'd been following me for the last week now. I could feel you." Ilan's voice softened as the lion drew near enough for him to touch. Which he did, holding out his palm for the lion to nuzzle. "Kurush, never do that to me again, okay?"

The lion said nothing. The lion could not speak. But its garnet eyes were dull and tired, yet somehow flickered deep down with a glow Ilan had never seen before.

"I won't ever leave you and you won't ever leave me, okay?"

The lion only sat on his striated silver haunches and stared at Ilan.

"Okay good. Glad we understand each other." Ilan said as he stood up with a groan. The mountains of blue diamonds and ice drew his gaze like a fire in the night. "Because we've still got a long road ahead of us."

ACKNOWLEDGMENTS

Finishing a novel is a unique feeling, and if it could be summed up in one word, that word would be gratitude. So many things happen throughout the course of writing a book, and to come to the end of the journey leaves me even more thankful than when I began. Just a few words in the back of a book can't really sum it all up, and any words I can provide are only a drop in the bucket to the true gratitude that is in my heart.

To Almighty God and His Son Jesus Christ, thank you for your love and grace and mercy. Thank you for giving me this story and the opportunity to tell it.

To my family, thank you for your love, patience, and all of your support. Thank you for your inspiration, for keeping me in balance, and keeping me humble, always. Thank you for being behind me from the very first word to the last.

To Laura Gordon, thank you for another perfect cover. We all judge a book by its cover and you always give my work a wonderful first impression by the skill of your work.

To Julie Eshbaugh, thank you for being the best writer friend a writer could have. You are amazing.

To Sveta, thank you for everything. I couldn't have written this without you.

To Amber, for being a wonderful librarian, proofreader, and friend.

To Yelena Lugin, thank you for your enthusiasm and support and lending your dog to this adventure.

To Rose Reid and Rebecca McNutt, thank you for your friendship and being there to talk about things writers need to talk about, and for being the first to always write reviews and support my work. You are both a blessing.

To Roshani Chokshi, thank you for being a rainbow of inspiration to me as an artist, and for being so kind as a human being. Please never stop writing.

To James A. Moore, thank you for being the benchmark for fantasy and for being such a good friend.

To Emily Murphy, thank you for being a wonderful friend and letting me read your beautiful debut.

To Lashaan & Trang of Bookidote.com, you guys are truly the greatest bloggers on the planet and are amazing bibliophiles and great friends. Thank you for your friendship and support. I hope you like the graphic novel just as much or better than the book and that it will be worth the wait for you both.

To Jackie, Kelly, and Lauren, thank you for your enthusiasm, support, and encouragement. I hope you all love this one just as much if not more than VoD. Thank you Lonna, Anja, Luna, and Yamina for supporting me and my work all across the globe!

To Oliver James, thank you for creating such a perfect font for the Woven Worlds series.

To Jason and Marina, thank you for your work on the ebook. You two are the best!

To Meshuggah, Jinjer, Chevelle, In Flames, InGhosts, Trivium, Insomnium, Dark Tranquility, Firewind, Trees of Eternity, and Lady Gaga for the soundtrack to Ozmander. As a writer, I am most certainly synesthetic, and your sounds and stories, colors and textures, and musical masterpieces truly helped me translate the story from my imagination to the page.

Finally, thank you, whoever you may be, for reading. Your support means a lot to me, whether by word of mouth or leaving a review of some kind, but just the fact that you read the story and enjoyed it and got something out of it or that it may've given something to you or blessed you or encouraged you or entertained you is more than enough for me.

72606132R00144

Made in the USA
Columbia, SC
21 June 2017